OF MICE AND MURDER

CAT AND MOUSE WHODUNITS 2

EMILY JAMES

STRONGHOLD BOOKS

ALSO BY EMILY JAMES

Maple Syrup Mysteries

Sapped: A Maple Syrup Mysteries Prequel

A Sticky Inheritance

Bushwhacked

Almost Sleighed

Murder on Tap

Deadly Arms

Capital Obsession

Tapped Out

Bucket List

End of the Line

Slay Bells Ringing

(also contains a Cupcake Truck Mystery novella)

Rooted in Murder

Guilty or Knot

Stumped

Cupcake Truck Mysteries

Sugar and Vice

Dead Velvet Cake

Gum Drop Dead

1

―――――

"Wait, Zoe! I need to borrow a cat."

Avery scurried across the yard, her beads and crystals bouncing against her chest and her long, flowing multi-colored skirts hiked up to show her bare feet. She waved her hand in the air. As if I might not see her if she didn't flag me down.

She needed to what? Did I have water clogging my ears from my morning shower? Or was *cat* short-form for something else I wasn't aware of?

I balanced my travel mug on the roof of my car and glanced at the time on my cell phone. I had enough wiggle room to make it to the veterinary clinic for work without being late as long as I didn't have to fend off another attempt by Avery to realign my chi or my chakras or whatever her latest new-age thing was. You'd have thought after three months of living next door to each other she'd have figured out that I wasn't game.

Avery huffed to a stop in front of me and bent over

slightly, hands on thighs. "Yoga doesn't do much for my cardio."

"You're welcome to start walking Orion if you'd like. He can always use more exercise. He still forgets the difference between the furniture and a chew toy when he's cooped up too long." *Don't look at your phone again. It's not very neighborly.* "I'm headed to work right now, but we can set up some walking times later if you'd like."

There. That was a subtle but clear hint, wasn't it? Diplomacy always felt so unnatural to me. The world would be a much better place if people just said what they meant. Then again, there'd also be a lot more people with their noses out of joint. Which probably explained why the rest of my family said I needed to at least work on developing tact outside of work.

Avery waved her hand at me. "I appreciate the offer, but I don't need a dog. I need a cat."

Oh boy. I hadn't heard wrong after all. "A cat?"

She bobbed her head, and her teal feather earrings brushed her shoulders. "I need to borrow one."

Borrow one? Nope, there was no subtle, tactful way to respond to that. "Cats aren't like cars. You can't rent a living being."

"Oh, I know that." Avery pressed her hands over her heart as if my words had stabbed her there. "I'm vegan. I don't support the exploitation of any animal. But I don't need a cat permanently. Just for a week or so. I thought the shelter might be able to loan me one."

I closed my eyes and took two deep breathes. Losing my temper wouldn't get me out of this conversation and to work any faster. "The shelter doesn't loan out cats. They're sentient creatures with feelings. Transitions are scary and confusing, and it's not fair to a cat to bring it home if you don't plan to keep it." I retrieved my travel mug from the car's roof. Hint, hint. I needed to get going. "You can always ask Judith when she gets home tonight in case I'm wrong, though."

Since Judith and I both worked in the animal care field, maybe she'd forgotten that my sister was the one who managed the local shelter, and I was the veterinarian.

Avery smiled beatifically at me. "Judith's got so much on her plate with her physio, and you're here now. I was hoping we could just take care of it rather than burdening her since you work at the shelter, too. Please?"

I didn't work at the shelter. Not technically. As Arbor's only veterinarian, I worked *with* the shelter, providing medical care for the animals brought in. Though, I guess if we were being technical about it, I had worked on the weekends very part time to help out while Judith was recovering from her broken leg.

I sighed. There seemed to be only one way to end this conversation. Face the crazy head on. "What do you need a cat for?"

Avery raised up on her toes and lowered down. She glanced over her shoulder as if she didn't want anyone overhearing. "I have a *mouse*." She whispered the words in the same hurried, embarrassed tone that someone else might say to their doctor *I have a fungus on my unmentionable parts*. "I found droppings in my cupboard."

If this was a sign of the way this day was going to go, I would need a *lot* more coffee. "You don't need a temporary cat. You need a mouse trap. You can get those from the hardware store. No adoption application necessary. Just add peanut butter."

I cringed internally. That had probably been a bit snarky even for me. But honestly. This conversation was ridiculous, and I was officially going to be late for work. I reached for the car door handle.

Avery grabbed my forearm with both her hands. Her mouth hung open as if I'd asked her to eat the mouse after trapping it. "I can't do that. I don't believe in killing unless it's the natural cycle of life."

Well, at least now her desire to borrow a cat made sense. Though, if we were going to get nit-picky about it, killing wasn't part of the natural cycle of life. Death didn't come into the world until after Adam and Eve rebelled against God, and humans and animals were all vegetarian until after the flood, when something in the environment must have changed to make eating meat necessary.

None of that was going to convince Avery to get a mouse trap, though. She only believed in God in a vague "some greater power in the universe" sense. She'd never read the Bible. She said it was too long.

My phone rang. Probably Maeve asking why I wasn't at work. I held up a finger in a one-second gesture to Avery. At least this would buy me some thinking time.

I pulled my phone out. Judith's picture and phone number filled the screen. Thank goodness. "It's Judith.

How about we ask her? She's the final authority when it comes to the shelter's animals."

Avery released her grip on my arm.

I swiped a finger across the screen. "Hey, Jude. I'm here with Avery. Is it okay if I put you on speaker?"

"He's bleeding." Judith's voice was thin and an octave too high. "I need you. The shelter."

My stomach lurched, and my brain shifted into triage mode. Whoever brought the animal in should have taken it straight to the veterinary clinic rather than the shelter if it was bleeding enough to make Judith sound that way. The shelter wasn't equipped for anything major. We'd have to stabilize him before we could transport him. Hopefully he was small and easy to move.

I mouthed the word *emergency* to Avery and climbed into my car. Not the way I would have chosen to get out of the conversation. "I'm on my way. What kind of wound?"

"I'm not sure." Her voice cracked. Was she crying? "I think he was shot, but he might've been stabbed. There's so much blood."

My heartbeat kicked up so high it hurt. Judith was a professional, same as me. We might break down after, but we didn't panic when we had an animal who needed our help on our hands. "I'm less than a minute away. What happened?"

"I don't know. I found him this way. There's so much blood. There's so much blood, Zo."

My throat closed, and I sent up a wordless prayer. She'd found him? Had someone simply abandoned the poor thing at the shelter door? That made no sense. "Dog or cat?"

"Bob." She was crying so hard her words were barely legible now. "It's Bob."

A hard shiver wracked my body from head to toe. Bob Bremnes, animal control officer for the shelter and Judith's friend.

I pressed my foot down on the gas, passing by the speed limit and continuing to pick up acceleration until the trees alongside the road were a green blur.

2

"**D**id you call 911?" I asked Judith through the phone.

"Right before I called you." She sniffled. "They're still waiting on the landline with me, on speaker."

I spun my car into the animal shelter parking lot. My tires squealed in a way that usually only happened in movies. Two other vehicles parked in the lot—Judith's car and Bob's. Had I gotten here before the emergency vehicles? I had been a lot closer. The ambulance base and the police station were on the complete opposite side of town. Even speeding, they could be five or ten minutes behind me.

"Are you almost here?" Judith's tone sounded like she was held together with nothing more solid than broken paperclips.

I jumped out of my car, leaving the door hanging open. "I'm here. I'm coming in."

Another woman's voice, too faint for me to hear the

words, spoke on Judith's end. Probably the 911 dispatcher updating her on the emergency vehicles. Judith could have been asking the question of either of us.

I sprinted across the pavement and into the shelter. "Judith?"

"Back here! We're back here!"

I ran through the shelter and into the area where the cats were kenneled at night. The acrid scent of dirty litter boxes hit my nose. Cats meowed from all sides, some sticking paws through the bars of their cages as I passed. Bob hadn't gotten far into the morning routine before it happened. The cart used to transport food at meal times was fully stocked and near the back of the room.

Right in front of the cart, feet stuck out from the end of the second last aisle. Black men's running shoes, toes pointing up as if the person were lying on their back. I skidded to a stop at the end of them.

Judith knelt on the ground next to Bob's body, her crutches dropped haphazardly on the floor. Her phone lay next to her, as did the landline handset. She pressed both hands over a red stain on Bob's shoulder-upper chest area. Blood coated her hands.

She'd been right. There was a lot of blood. Not only on her hands and Bob's clothes, but seeping out from underneath him, too. His clothes didn't look torn. A bullet wound then.

My throat and mouth dried out. I dropped down beside Judith.

She turned wide eyes toward me. "I don't understand. Why would someone do this?"

I shook my head and glanced at Bob. His eyes were closed. His skin had an unnatural gray tinge.

Was he still breathing? I put a hand over Judith's, as if to help her. Her hands rose slightly underneath mine.

Thank you, God. He was still alive.

But he might not make it until the ambulance arrived. Not with this much blood loss. For all we knew, the bullet had hit an artery. If he'd been a dog or a cat, I could have been more confident about the potential damage. Their arteries were more familiar to me than my own phone number.

I needed to get Judith out of here in case he didn't survive long enough for real help to reach us. I had to protect her from this. I was the big sister. "I'll put pressure on his wound. My arms are fresh. You need to go out front and wait for the ambulance. Show them exactly where we are so they don't have to search, okay?"

Judith nodded, and I swapped my hands for hers, pressing one down on top of the other and leaning my weight in slightly. Warm, sticky blood oozed between my fingers. I could do a better job if I had a piece of material to staunch the bleeding, but it wasn't far enough into fall to need to wear a jacket. And I couldn't risk taking the pressure off long enough to strip my scrub top off.

Judith was struggling to get a hold on her crutches. She pushed herself up to her feet, taking them with her.

"Throw me a towel," I said.

Her face went paler than should have been possible. "I should have thought of that."

I lifted my hands, and she quickly shoved the towel

underneath. I pushed down again with my full body weight this time. "You couldn't have done it by yourself."

She didn't need any guilt over this. It was hard enough for me to think clearly, and I wasn't as close to Bob as she was.

A faint sound that might have been a siren reached my ears. Bob's breathing grew shallower under my hands. "I think the ambulance is coming. You'd better go."

Judith hobbled out of the room, swinging her crutches so fast it couldn't have been safe. I prayed out loud. Maybe Bob could still hear me somehow, and he'd be comforted by it.

What could have been ten minutes or only one later, two men rolled a stretcher through the doors, asking Judith questions as they went. She hopped along behind them.

They deftly moved me out of the way. Their actions spun together—cutting open his shirt, binding the wound, inserting an IV, snapping an oxygen mask over his face. I scooped up the landline handset and told the 911 dispatcher that the ambulance had arrived, and the paramedics got Bob onto the stretcher.

Then Judith and I were standing alone, a puddle of blood at our feet.

The sounds and smells and slickness on my hands were far away and tinny. Like I was watching them on TV. I saw blood every day. My stomach shouldn't feel like it was trying to crawl up into my throat.

The siren from the ambulance faded, and other distant sirens drew closer. The police would be here any second to secure the scene. They'd have to look for evidence of who did this. They'd want to take our statements and our fingerprints and our DNA, so they could know what we left behind and what might belong to the intruder.

But I didn't want to stand here staring at Bob's blood until they came. If I threw up, I'd contaminate the scene. What I wouldn't give to go back to when I thought Avery pestering me for a loaner cat was going to be the worst part of my day. "We should wait outside."

Silence answered me. I forced my gaze away from the red on the floor and onto Judith. Her expression was unnaturally flat, her eyes focused on nothing.

"Judith." Trying to keep my voice strong and steady was like trying to hold two sides of ripped fabric together while the threads unraveled beneath my fingers. "We're going outside now."

Her head dipped fractionally. I moved for the door, and she followed, her crutches hitting the ground unevenly, as if she were struggling to control them.

We stepped out the front door.

Another car had parked in the parking lot next to my car, which still had the driver's side door hanging open. At least I'd remembered to turn it off. I was pretty sure I had.

Two police cruisers sat to the left with officers clustered around them. Their sirens were off, but their lights were still blipping colors, visible even in the daylight.

"I should have gone with him. In the ambulance." Judith's voice sounded as disconnected as I felt. Her hands clenched around the handles of her crutches, making her knuckles jut out like a row of miniature boulders. "How am I supposed to know what's happening to him if I'm not there?"

There or not wouldn't matter. She wasn't next of kin. The doctors wouldn't tell her anything even if she was underfoot the whole time. "Do you know how to contact his family?"

She stared in the direction the ambulance had gone. "He doesn't have...I'm his emergency contact. I'm...I need to be there."

They were closer friends than I'd realized if he'd made her his emergency contact.

I just needed to get enough air into my lungs, and then I could figure this out for her. We could solve this. I drew in a breath until my lungs hurt. I eased it out.

She needed to be at the hospital. We could fix that.

I took her shoulder and turned her toward my car. "We're going to the hospital. I'll drive you there."

Judith blinked rapidly, as if she were struggling to make sense of my words. "We can't leave. The police will have questions."

I nudged her, and she moved like I had a video game controller and was pushing her buttons. "They can find you there."

Detective Ryan MacIntosh stepped out of the group of officers. His charcoal suit accentuated his broad shoulders, and he'd added just enough gel to his dark, curly hair to make it behave—something my wavy hair never seemed willing to do no matter how much product I applied.

We hadn't been quick enough. Now I was going to have to somehow talk him into letting us leave.

He strode toward us. "Dr. Stephenson. How is it that you end up at so many crime scenes covered in blood?"

"One crime scene. Two counting this one. Two isn't *many*." My voice sounded funny, all wavery and small.

Something flickered over his face that I couldn't decipher, a quick tightening of the muscles around his lips. "Are either of you hurt?"

I shook my head and glanced at Judith. She shook her head. Her eyes looked glazed again.

I put a hand on her shoulder and gave a tiny push toward my car. "I'm going to drive Judith to the hospital, though, so she can answer any questions the doctors have about Bob. She's his emergency contact."

Detective MacIntosh stepped in front of us. "You can't drive her to the hospital."

"I'll come back as soon as I drop her off, so you don't need to worry that we're fleeing the scene." My words were coming out too fast, running all together, and I couldn't seem to stop them. "Someone still needs to take care of the animals. And an officer can go to the hospital to ask Judith questions."

"That's not what I mean." His voice wasn't harsh or demanding the way I'd expected it to be when I told him we planned to leave the scene of a crime. He directed his gaze at my right hand. "You can't drive right now. It wouldn't be safe. You're both in shock."

Crazy talk. I was absolutely fine. I just needed to take care of Judith. That meant getting her to the hospital to be near Bob. Then everything would be fine.

I followed his pointed gaze to my hand. I'd been rubbing it against my scrub pants without realizing it, smearing more blood all over my clothes, as if subconsciously trying to wipe Bob's blood off my skin. I held my hand numbly out in front of me. It shook. Why did it feel like it wasn't even my hand?

Detective MacIntosh cupped a hand around my elbow. "Get in my car. I'll drive you both there so a doctor can look at you too."

Judith hobbled after us on her crutches as if she were attached to me by a rope.

Maybe he had a point. Judith was acting like my reflection in a mirror, moving only when I moved, and my body felt like it belonged to a stranger, so copying me wasn't the best idea.

"Okay," I said. "We wanted to go there anyway."

A smile whispered across Detective MacIntosh's lips. "Don't worry. I'm not naïve enough to think you're going because I asked you to."

"Good." I flopped down into the passenger seat of his car. The shaking from my hand had spread down my body into my legs. "As long as that's clear."

Detective MacIntosh leaned over and snapped my seat belt into place as if I were a small child. "Absolutely clear."

3

I'd just finished packing a change of clothes to take to the hospital for Judith after work when the doorbell rang.

I zipped the backpack closed and slung it over my shoulder. It had to be Avery back again. She must have noticed my car in the driveway and decided to pick our conversation up where we'd left off this morning. She'd have to wait until tonight. After going to the hospital, finally being cleared by a doctor, and coming home to wash the blood off and change, I'd already needed Maeve to reschedule all my morning appointments.

I stormed down the stairs. "No, Avery." I flung open the door. "You can't hire a cat the way other people would hire an exterminator."

My words petered off at the end. I stood facing a man's chest, decked out in a crisp white dress shirt and navy tie.

I raised my gaze. Keith. The anger and tension dropped off my shoulders. "You're not Avery."

The edges of his mouth tilted up, but the tension lines stayed between his eyes. "Definitely not Avery. All those bracelets and beads would drive me crazy."

He opened his arms, and I set down the backpack and stepped into them. I buried my face into his shirt. He always smelled so good, like laundry soap and sandalwood. At least I didn't smell meaty like blood anymore.

His hold tightened slightly. "Maeve wanted me to check on you. She said when you called her to reschedule your morning you were babbling something about blood in your hair."

His hand touched my towel-wrapped head.

I cringed. For once, it'd be nice for him to see me not looking like a walking disaster zone. And, of course, Maeve would have to describe my—admittedly—disjointed phone call as babbling. I wasn't babbling. She'd have had trouble pulling her thoughts together too if she'd had someone's blood pumping through her fingers a half hour before.

If I didn't get my act together, though, Keith wasn't going to want to continue dating me. A pastor needed someone who looked like they had their life together. No, strike that. A pastor needed someone who had their life together. Someone who could be a good example for others. It was only a matter of time before he figured out that wasn't me.

I stepped back. "Did she call you as my pastor or as my boyfriend?"

"A little of both, I think. Though she wasn't clear about why you had blood in your hair. I had images of you with a head wound."

There was a haunted tone to his words when he said *head wound*, and the lines between his eyes deepened. If it weren't for the way he still wore his hair cropped short, it'd be easy to forget he'd once been a military chaplain, regularly deployed overseas. He didn't like to talk about what he'd seen, but it wasn't a stretch to believe head wounds might have been part of it.

"It wasn't my blood." Though it had taken three rounds of shampoo before I'd felt like I might be clean again.

I took the towel off my head, shook out my hair to help reassure him, and gave him the full story—obviously in a much more coherent way than I'd given to Maeve earlier.

"I'm not sure that makes it any better." He sucked in a deep breath. "I thought small towns weren't supposed to have the same crime rate as bigger cities."

That wasn't really a fair comparison. Even with the recent murder of Sebastian Clunes and now the attack on Bob, Arbor wasn't anywhere near as dangerous as someplace like Detroit. But now that we were becoming a bedroom community for a couple of the cities an hour's drive away, it was inevitable that we'd see at least a small uptick in crime.

Keith was still looking at me like even being in the same building where a crime took place was too close a call. A tight feeling scratched around inside my chest.

Shouldn't I have been the one to think to call him? He shouldn't have had to hear about me being covered in blood from Maeve. That wasn't what a good girlfriend would do.

I took his hand and squeezed it. "I'm fine. I promise."

He rolled his shoulders and seemed to wipe the worry lines from his face by force. "You might not be if you're much later getting into work. Maeve also said something about you owing her for leaving her alone with Tyler all morning? Is Tyler a dog who won't stop barking or something?"

I stifled a snort-laugh. "Tyler's the new vet tech, the one we hired after Lisa found out she was pregnant again and decided to quit to be a stay-at-home mom."

The look of confusion on Keith's face was adorable. For a few moments at least, it made him look like a little boy. "And why doesn't she want to be alone with him?"

I bit my bottom lip, but even that couldn't hold back my smirk. "Tyler's a bit of a flirt. And the more Maeve rebuffs him, the more fun he finds it to flirt with her."

"She shot down the idea again of hiring Kat back?"

The mirth drained out of me, and I nodded. Maeve and I had both pleaded for leniency at Kat's sentencing trial, resulting in her getting only two months in jail for her theft. Even though she was out on probation now, Maeve refused to even consider rehiring her. And apparently my status as official partner in the business didn't mean I had a veto vote. The agreement we'd made was that we both had to want to hire each new employee we brought on since we'd both need to work with them. Maeve said she could never trust Kat again.

Her inability to forgive Kat and give her a second chance sat in my stomach like I'd eaten rocks. If she couldn't forgive Kat, had she actually been able to move past my indiscretions at my past job or deep down did she not trust me either?

I sighed. "I'd better get going before she fires him. We need to bring on more staff, not lose the one we have."

I helped set up the details for a cat's dental surgery, then went back into the exam room to wipe things down. That was officially the last appointment for the day. I could finally head to the hospital to sit with Judith. Her last text had said that Bob had survived surgery. The silence since then had made me jump every time a client's phone dinged with a text or rang with a call.

The exam room door opened and closed.

Tyler leaned against it and tossed an apple back and forth between his hands. "So, if I invited Maeve out to dinner, you think she'd go?"

What was it about being in a relationship that seemed to make everyone else think you were a good source for advice? He wasn't going to like what I had to say since I was going to say the same thing I'd said the last five times he'd asked me. "You seem to have selective amnesia. Her fiancé died three months ago."

He crunched down on the apple. "I'm happy to be her rebound."

I rolled my eyes. He was at least five years younger than Maeve and me. Maybe he really didn't get it. "She wasn't dumped. I don't think people have rebound relationships after someone dies."

He shrugged and took another oversized bite of his apple. "She's too beautiful to spend so much time crying. That's all I'm saying."

Maeve was that. She could've gotten a side hustle as a Reese Witherspoon double.

My phone pinged, and I leaped for it.

Bob's awake. The police are on their way to talk to him.

I sighed out a breath, and my shoulders loosened. Awake had to be a positive sign. Plus, maybe Bob saw his attacker, and this could all be over. Whatever came next, I should head to the hospital to be there for Judith. At the very least, she'd want her fresh clothes. She'd refused to go home and clean up, wanting to stay at the hospital in case there was any change in Bob's condition, for better or worse, after the surgery.

I stuffed my phone into my pocket and tossed the bottle of cleaner at Tyler. He caught it with one hand while continuing to eat his apple. Some people got all the skills.

He might be right about Maeve spending too much time crying, but someone who didn't take her grief seriously also wasn't right for her. Grief wasn't something you could put a time limit on. Three months was barely any time when you lost the person you thought you'd spend your whole life with. All the flirting was funny at first, but he was taking things too far. A guy like him was only going to end up hurting her heart more.

"I've got to go to the hospital. You can finish cleaning up." I pointed a finger at Tyler. "You're a great vet tech, but Maeve's my friend. She's asked you to leave her alone. It's time you respected that, or *I'll* have to fire you like she keeps threatening to. Understand?"

He choked slightly and swallowed hard as if trying to move a lump of wedged apple down his throat. "Yes, ma'am."

4
_____

Judith and I stood with hands clasped outside Bob's hospital room. I'd tried to argue that Judith should be allowed to stay in the room while the police took Bob's statement, but Detective MacIntosh closed the door in my face.

With Judith still needing crutches and refusing to release my hand, I couldn't even pace the hallway. "Have you been able to see him yet?"

Judith bobbed her head. "But he was too groggy to speak. As soon as I told the nurses he was awake, they kicked me out. Ryan's orders. He didn't want Bob discussing what happened with anyone else before he spoke to him. He said that the first time a witness tells their story is usually the most accurate because they haven't gotten any outside feedback to slant things."

Her voice wasn't resentful the way mine would have been. "It's ridiculous. It's not like you're going to lead his answers."

She squeezed my hand. "It's not ridiculous. Bob can't hold anything back because he's afraid of upsetting me or frightening me."

I used my free hand to do a quick search on my phone about whether it was normal for police to keep witnesses separate until they'd taken their statements. The first page I checked said that was normal procedure. Witnesses who spoke to each other would naturally coordinate their stories without realizing it. If one person was convinced the perpetrator wore a baseball cap, for example, and the others hadn't seen a hat, they might start to remember a hat where there hadn't been one.

I checked two more pages. They both agreed with the first. I huffed out a breath. Fine. Maybe Detective MacIntosh wasn't being unreasonable. That didn't mean he wasn't still obnoxious.

The door to Bob's room opened, and Detective MacIntosh emerged with another detective.

"Thanks for being so patient, Judith." Detective MacIntosh stopped next to us. "He's anxious to see you, so we'll get out of your way. Let me know if there's anything you need."

She smiled at him as if he'd given her the one thing she'd wanted most for Christmas. "Thanks, Ryan. I appreciate you taking this so seriously."

The smile he gave in return was probably meant to be comforting, but combined with his crooked nose, it transformed his otherwise average face into unnaturally handsome. Like a reformed rogue. Something I shouldn't notice. I had a boyfriend. A nice, non-annoying boyfriend.

His gaze landed on me, and the smile faded. He jutted his chin in a mockery of a greeting. "Dr. Stephenson."

He strode off down the hall, motioning the other detective to follow him.

Something tight wrapped around my throat. He liked Judith; he didn't like me. He'd made that abundantly clear the first few times we'd met when he'd made sure to rub Tonya's incarceration in my face and suggest that her crimes were enough reason to suspect that I'd killed Sebastian. Like mother like daughter, after all.

Which was fine. I didn't like him either, and Judith was nicer than me. She always had been. But would it have killed him to not make his dislike so obvious? It was humiliating. Especially since we went to the same church.

Judith tugged her hand free and tucked her crutches against her sides. "Come on." Her smile was so stunning it was like looking into a solar flare.

I followed Judith into Bob's room. She went straight to the chair next to his bed.

Someone had propped Bob up with a couple pillows behind his back, probably so that he didn't have to give his statement to the police while looking up at them from a prone position. A sling supported his arm. His hazel eyes were sunken in his face, and his skin carried a faint blue-gray cast. It made the gray strands in his brown hair more noticeable. I hadn't thought he had so many before.

An IV drip and an oxygen meter were still connected to him, and that faint disinfectant odor that always hung around hospitals was nearly overpowering.

I'd dealt with one gunshot wound at the clinic I worked at in the city, so my knowledge was pretty limited, but that case taught me that surviving the surgery was only the first step. Gunshot wounds introduced foreign matter into the body that could lead to an infection. Bob wasn't safe yet.

"I'm glad you waited." His voice grated like sandpaper, and he glanced at me. "Both of you. The nurse told me I wouldn't have made it without you two."

My eyes burned, and the back of my throat pinched shut. The warm, sticky sensation of Bob's blood on my hands shoved to the front of my mind. I shook my hands out. Now was not the time to break down. "It was mostly Judith."

Judith shook her head. "Zoe's the one who thought of using a towel to help stop the bleeding."

He chuckled. "You two really are two peas in a pod."

Warmth flooded into my center. He might be the only one to think Judith and I were alike, but I wasn't going to disabuse him of the notion.

Being lumped together with Judith cut off my instinctive next question about whether he remembered anything about his attacker. Judith wouldn't leap into that. "How do you feel?"

He gave his bandaged shoulder a pointed look. "About as well as I can considering someone put a hole through me. The doctor said I was lucky the bullet went all the way through. They can do more damage if they break apart inside. Ryan says that actually gives us a lead, too, even though they didn't find the bullet. They know it likely wasn't a hollow point because those usually fracture, he said. The gun might have been an older weapon. Pre-1980s, he said."

An old weapon seemed like a strange choice for a random intruder. Anyone who couldn't legally buy a gun would probably get one off the black market, and those would be new. So maybe the gun was something they'd stolen in a prior robbery? That might be helpful too. If the police found fingerprints at the shelter from the intruder, they might be able to match them to other crimes already in the database.

Judith shuddered, but Bob seemed calm as he told us everything Detective MacIntosh had said. Maybe that was because he'd been unconscious while Judith had a mind full of memories of him lying bleeding on the floor of the animal shelter. She'd see that again every time she went into shelter for a very long time.

At least, I would.

A chill slithered over my skin, and I wrapped my arms around my middle. The sooner the police caught whoever did this, the better. "Were you able to tell the police anything that might help them catch the shooter?"

Bob's shoulders started to rise in a shrug. He sucked in a breath, and the remaining color drained from his face. "Have to remember not to do that for a while."

Judith made a strangled sound. She put a hand over her face, but tears leaked out from underneath.

"Hey." Bob's voice was soft enough that I almost felt like I was eavesdropping on something private. "I'm like a tough old turkey. No one seriously considers turning him into soup because he'd be too chewy."

I snickered and clapped a hand over my mouth. Bob winked at me.

Judith gave a snuffling laugh and lowered her hand. "That makes no sense."

"No, but it made you smile again."

Her smile grew. "And you're not that old."

I twisted my hands in front of me while they talked. Bob had moved the conversation away from what had happened and onto making sure the animals at the shelter were taken care of. Judith obviously couldn't handle more talk of the attack right now.

But I needed to know. If I went home without more information, it'd be like trying to sleep next to an airport with all the ideas flying around in my head.

I picked up the backpack I'd brought for Judith. "I need to head home to take care of Orion, but why don't you sneak to the restroom and change while I'm still here to sit with Bob?"

Judith glanced down at her clothes as if just realizing her jeans and shirt were still spattered with Bob's blood. The expression on her face said she couldn't believe she'd been so insensitive as to not change already. "Good idea."

She slid the backpack on and left.

I sank into the empty chair.

Most of the animation had drained from Bob's face. His head slumped back against the pillows mounded up behind him. He might be asleep again before Judith got back. "You're still curious?"

I nodded.

He smoothed the blanket over his lap. "I didn't have much useful to tell the police. I think it was a man. He was taller than most women, about my height, and he moved like a man. But he had one of those snowmobile masks on, and he didn't say anything, so I can't be sure. I can't even remember if he wore gloves or not."

My heart tripped inside my chest. Judith could have easily been the one to arrive first. She could easily have shown up when the man was still there. "He didn't say anything? No demand for money or drugs?"

Bob shook his head. "I went into the back to start the morning routine. Loaded up the cart with food and medications. I heard the door open, thought it was Judith, and turned around to say hello. He was standing there. I tried to get away. That might be why he shot me. Maybe he thought I was going to set off an alarm or something." He twitched slightly as if he'd intended to shrug his shoulders and remembered not to right before he followed through. "I don't remember anything after the gunshot."

The snowmobile mask suggested the man planned to do something illegal. He hadn't wanted to risk anyone seeing his face. Unfortunately, it could mean he hadn't intended to kill Bob, or it could mean that he had but simply hadn't wanted to risk any witnesses seeing his face.

Bob also didn't sound like he knew why someone would have wanted to shoot him.

What he'd told the police really wasn't much to go on. Hopefully Detective MacIntosh was on the top of his game. I wasn't the only person in Arbor who wasn't going to feel safe as long as another almost-murderer was running loose.

5

My phone rang as I walked back out to my car, and I flinched. *Please God, let it not be bad news about Bob.* Even though I'd only left him and Judith a few minutes ago, any number of things could have happened in that length of time. He could have lost consciousness. He could have had a heart attack. He could have thrown a stroke-inducing blood clot.

Or was I about to get called into an after-hours emergency at the vet clinic? Those were always the worst—the animals who couldn't wait until we opened in the morning.

You're catastrophizing, the sensible side of me said. *It could be a telemarketer instead.*

What did that say about the day I'd had that I was hoping a telemarketer was calling me?

I sucked in a long, deep breath and pulled out my phone. My eyes were gritty, and the number on the screen blurred. I blinked rapidly, and it came into focus.

Foreign.

See. Telemarketer.

I shoved my phone back into my purse.

My heart shot up into my throat. No, today was Monday. Monday evening—the time Mom and Dad usually called.

I grabbed the phone back out of my purse and swiped a finger across the screen right before it went to voicemail. "Hello?"

"Zoe?"

The line crackled, but I'd recognize my dad's voice anywhere. A voice so big and strong that he almost hadn't needed a microphone when he preached. A voice that filled a room and couldn't be toned down even by being halfway across the world on a bad connection. A voice that immediately brought to mind broken bikes and skinned knees and him saying, "It'll be okay. We can fix it."

I burst into tears—the ugly cry kind. As if I'd stored all the stress and worry of the day up inside, and now it was exploding like a can of hairspray left in direct sunlight.

Between blowing my nose into a tissue and gasping for air, I told our parents what happened.

"We'll call Judith next." Mom's voice had the no-need-to-panic tone that used to make me want to throw something at her when we'd first met, back when I referred to her as *Camille, the stepmother I never wanted.* My child-brain interpreted her composure as judgment, like she was implying that I was always overreacting or too emotional.

Now it made me wish she were here so I could hug her and let her unflappable calm wrap around me. It made me wish I was more like her. She wouldn't be sobbing in the middle of a parking lot like some lunatic.

"Do you need us to come home?" she asked as if she could read my mind across the thousands of miles separating us. "A lot seems to be happening. If you need us, we'll be on a flight tomorrow."

I opened my mouth to say *yes*. To say that I didn't want to have to handle all of this anymore. That I didn't want to have to be a grown-up. Why was it that as a kid I'd always thought being a grown-up would be better than being a child, but once I hit adulthood, I would have given up almost anything to have even one day without adult responsibilities? Was it a natural part of humanity to want whatever we didn't have and not appreciate what we did? Because as a child I couldn't drink coffee, and there was something to be said for that.

"Zoe? Did we lose the connection?"

"Still here." I unlocked my car and climbed inside. At least then someone wouldn't come out of the hospital, see me blubbering, and think someone died. "Stay where you are. We've got this."

"You're sure?" my dad asked.

The parking lot around me was full of vehicles but devoid of people, so I rolled down the windows of my car. The crisp evening air seemed to blow away all the dandelion fluff clogging my brain. They couldn't do anything to help here even if they came home.

Plus, I didn't want them to feel like they had to put their lives on hold to take care of me—to take care of Judith too, but really me, since I was the one they always had to worry about while Judith and I were growing up. I was the one who talked back to teachers, stole things, and probably caused my dad to lose all his hair before he turned thirty.

Who was I kidding? They probably still worried about me, between my bad relationship decisions, losing my previous job under questionable circumstances, and nearly getting myself killed by a murderer a few months back. My life choices so far couldn't possibly instill them with confidence that I was a competent adult.

If they came home now, they'd never feel like I could manage when they weren't around to protect me anymore.

They'd made so many sacrifices for me already. This missionary trip sabbatical was their dream. I was *not* going to take that from them. "Completely sure."

And even if I wasn't completely sure yet, I would find a way to be. Then they'd see I could take care of myself and make good choices. That I *was* making good choices. I was helping Judith while she recovered, I was a partner in my own business, and I was dating a pastor. Keith was exactly the kind of man they would want for me.

"I promise." I rolled up my windows and turned on my car. "You don't need to worry."

What was that noise? My alarm already?

I peeled open my eyes. Outside my window, the sky was still dark, the moon high and the streetlamps casting a soothing glow. Not morning. I rolled over, lining my gaze up with the bedside clock.

11:23 pm.

My phone then? Crap. A call this late at night couldn't be good.

I slapped a hand out and grabbed it off the bedside table. Avery's name rolled across my screen.

Was this a bad joke? Unless your house was on fire, you didn't call your neighbor after 9:00 pm, and we were well past that. Though, with Avery, it wouldn't surprise me if she didn't own a clock and instead told time by a sundial in her backyard.

I slid my finger across the screen. "Do you know what time it is?"

"Sorry. Sorry." Avery's voice sounded frazzled. "I do know. But my issue has gotten worse."

Her issue? I pressed the heel of one hand into the space between my eyes. She was acting like I should know exactly why she was calling, but the gears in my mind felt like they were chewing up wood. I could barely find words. What had I talked to her about last? Ohhh… "Is this about the mouse?"

"Yes." The word came out high-pitched and breathy. "He's chewing inside the walls by my bed right now."

If Jesus hadn't said to love your neighbor as yourself, I

would have hung up on her. Judith or my mom might have had the patience to deal with something like this, but I just wanted to shake her and see if it rattled loose some common sense. "Go sleep on your couch for the night. In the morning, if you need the moral support, I'll drive you to the store and I'll buy you mousetraps. I'll even set them up for you."

"I don't have a couch. You know that!"

I dropped my head back onto my pillow. That was right. She'd decided to feng shui her house, and apparently her couch had been pushing things out of alignment. Now all she had were bean bags and throw pillows around her coffee table. None of them were big enough to sleep on. They were barely big enough to sit on.

"Did you try banging on the wall to scare it away?"

Two loud thumps echoed through the phone. I pulled it away from my ear. I just wanted to sleep. Was that so wrong?

"He stopped for a few seconds then started back up again. I think he's building a nest in there. By tomorrow I could have a dozen mice. You have to help me. Please. The shelter must have a cat who could come live with me on a temporary basis."

I draped an arm above my head and settled in. Why had I thought this would be a short conversation? "The only time cats go to a home on a temporary basis is fostering."

"I'll do that then."

I sighed. "You said you only wanted a cat for as long as it took to catch the mouse. If you sign up to foster, you have to keep the cat until it finds a permanent home. Are you willing to commit to that?"

"Yes!"

The desperation in her voice created a mental image of her crouched on her bed with her arms wrapped over her ears, trying to block out the sounds of the mouse's chewing.

I sighed internally this time. I shouldn't be so hard on her really. It could push a person to the edge when all they wanted was sleep and something—or someone—kept waking them up. I should know. "We can go fill in all the paperwork first thing tomorrow before I go into the clinic."

I moved my finger toward the screen to tap the disconnect button.

"Wait, Zoe!" Her voice was up into the range that was almost beyond human hearing again, as if she could see me about to end the call. "I need the cat tonight. The mouse is chewing right now."

Was there a serenity prayer for when you just wanted to scream at people? Deep breath in, hold it, deep breath out. "A cat isn't a magic button. It won't catch the mouse the instant it's in the house. It'll have to wait until the mouse comes out of your walls."

"But it might smell the cat and decide to move to a cat-free house. I have to do something. It could be gnawing through electrical wires while we speak."

Which is why I suggested a mouse trap *this morning*.

Logic clearly wasn't going to win me this battle. "Are you prepared to cat-proof your house tonight? Put all your poisonous houseplants out of reach. Shut off your essential oil diffusers until you can check with me whether the oils they're sending into the air would be harmful to a cat if they got it on their fur and licked it off. Put away or make inaccessible your salt lamp."

"My salt lamp?" Her tone was confused now.

"Cats are known to get addicted to licking them, and it can cause salt toxicity."

"Oh." A pause. "Yes. Yes, I can do all that immediately. It's not like I'll be able to sleep if I don't get the cat anyway. Do you want to drive or should I?"

Keeping Avery on track was like trying to wrangle an easily-distracted toddler. How did she still have this level of energy in the middle of the night? It was unnatural.

"Avery," I called from the end of the row where she stood cooing at a litter of eight-week-old kittens, "those are babies. You'd be lucky if they could catch their own tail let alone a mouse. The ones you want are farther back."

As if to prove my point, the biggest of the kittens tried to reach for the finger Avery had poked through the bars and toppled over into his sister.

Avery sighed and withdrew her hand. "Are you sure? Maybe their size would let them get into spaces a bigger cat couldn't."

Their small size would absolutely do that, but not the way Avery hoped. Instead, it'd let them get stuck behind the washing machine. Then I'd be getting another call from her begging me to come to the rescue. "You need a full-grown cat."

I led her past the row where Bob had been shot. I held my breath and peeked at the floor. Clean just like Detective MacIntosh said it would be. I let the pent-up air out of my lungs.

On the drive to the hospital that morning, I'd been worried about the animals at the shelter. He'd promised they'd fast-track evidence collection, finishing within a couple of hours so a cleaning crew could deal with the blood and a shelter employee could feed and clean the animals.

Detective MacIntosh might be annoying, but he certainly kept his word. He'd done more than he needed to, in fact. According to Maeve, the shelter should have been responsible for contacting a crime scene cleaner to come in. When I'd texted Detective MacIntosh to ask how we found one of those, he'd said it was taken care of.

I moved the feeding cart to the side, out of our way, so we wouldn't have to wriggle past it. All the food was still on it. The shelter employee who came in to care for the animals must not have realized they could use it again. I could just imagine them tiptoeing around, trying not to touch anything they didn't absolutely need to touch for fear of contaminating the crime scene.

The crime scene. Not a phrase I could have ever imagined associating with the shelter.

A shiver skittered over my skin. The shadows cast by the lights at the front suddenly seemed deeper and longer, as if they meant to grab and hold us. I really should have turned all the lights on rather than trying to keep it dim for the animals. Then again, all the lights were on and the sun was shining when Bob was shot. Bright lights didn't automatically equal safety.

The sooner we got out of here, the better I'd feel.

I maneuvered Avery in front of the cage that held a large tabby male. He had big cheeks and a notch out of one ear, speaking to his previous outdoor life. He stared at us without blinking. "This is the one I think you should foster. He's had to hunt before. He'll know what to do with a mouse."

Avery squinted at his name tag. "Oscar? Like Oscar the Grouch?" She made a face. "I can't have that. He'll disrupt the harmony in my house."

I clenched my hands into fists. The older cats, the less aesthetically pleasing cats, and the black cats always had a harder time finding homes regardless of how perfect they might be for someone in every other respect. But I'd never heard of someone rejecting an animal based on the entirely temporary name we'd given them at the shelter. "He's not actually grumpy. He's a sweetheart."

She crinkled up her nose and wandered off, peering into the other cages. She stopped three spots down. "I want this one. Her name's Star. It's a sign."

I opened my mouth to ask how her being named Star could be a sign. I clamped it shut again. I didn't really want to know. Asking would only prolong this ordeal and keep me from my bed that much longer.

I moved next to Avery. The cat blinking at us from

inside the cage was petite with soft-looking silver fur. She was one of the cases where I couldn't help wondering what her story was. When her finder brought her in, she was already spayed, and she was clean and well-fed, suggesting someone had cared about her. She didn't look like a cat who'd been on their own long. Even when our microchip scanner didn't reveal a chip, both Judith and I expected someone to come looking for her during the three-day hold the shelter put on strays. No one had.

Her appeal for Avery was obvious. She was beautiful. She'd find a home fast. "I guess she is a good one to take if you don't want to foster long-term. Let's fill out the paperwork."

I put Star into the carrier I'd brought from home since Avery didn't have one. I handed Avery the carrier and grabbed a bag of food from the food cart on our way past. It was open, but it didn't look like Bob had used any out of it before he'd been shot, so it should be plenty to feed Star until she found her forever home.

A confused look passed over Avery's face. "Do I need that? I figured she'd just eat the mouse. That's the whole point, right?"

Heaven help me. I didn't have enough patience for this at my best, let alone when I was running on an hour of sleep. I lifted my gaze to the ceiling and counted the tiles until I could be sure I wasn't about to make the shelter the scene of a second murder. "Yes, Avery, you need to feed her every day. More than once in fact. And I will be checking."

Annoying sound. I pulled the covers up over my head. Too loud.

The sound burrowed into my warm sleep cocoon. My alarm? Still too dark.

Could it be…?

I groaned. My phone again. Twice in one night. I peeled my eyes open one at a time, the lids so heavy it took conscious effort.

2:03 am glowed on my digital clock. I'd been back in bed for less than two hours after dropping Avery and Star off.

If this was Avery calling again, asking me some question about the cat I just sent home with her, I was hanging up this time. I gave her everything she could possibly need. Even a litter box, a scooper, and some litter. If Star wasn't showing interest in her mouse problem, that was Avery's fault for picking her, and she was going to have to live with it.

I pulled the phone over and propped it on the bed next to me. It took me two swipes to answer with my eyes mostly closed. "No." My words came out slow and sleep garbled. "You can't swap cats."

Quiet on the other end. I could hear breathing.

"That must have been some dream you were having," Detective MacIntosh's voice finally said.

A jolt raced through my body, burning away the sleepiness. A police officer calling in the middle of the night. "Is Bob okay? What's going on?"

"Everyone's fine. I just need you to come down to the shelter. There's been a break-in, and we need someone to tell us if anything is missing. I thought you'd prefer I let Judith rest and call you instead."

I scrubbed a hand through my hair. That was actually thoughtful of him. But someone had dragged him out of bed tonight unnecessarily, too. "There wasn't a break in. I was there tonight placing a cat in foster care—long story. Whoever called in the break-in must have seen the car and the lights inside. I'm sorry someone called you out on a false alarm."

Even though it was Detective MacIntosh, I truly was sorry. I currently had sympathy for anyone who got dragged out of their bed in the middle of the night for something that could have waited until morning.

"I don't think that's it. Not unless you trashed the place, too."

6

Detective MacIntosh's unmarked vehicle and a regular squad car were parked outside the animal shelter when I pulled up.

Detective MacIntosh must have been waiting for me because he opened the door for me as I walked up. The lights inside the shelter had all been turned on. I blinked against the industrial brightness.

Trashed wasn't exactly the right word for what the intruder had done. They hadn't smashed any windows or graffitied any walls.

Papers were scattered all across the floor. The receptionist's rolling chair had been tipped over. Which, honestly, made no sense. That thing was heavy. The intruder couldn't have tipped it merely by bumping into it. Did they think we secretly hid the strong drugs in the lining or something? Joke was on them. The shelter kept only minimal medications on site—basically whatever was needed for the animals under care, which meant primarily things like antibiotics, eye and ear drops, and skin creams.

They'd even swept Avery's foster home paperwork off the counter. It was now somewhere in the mess on the floor rather than where we'd left it. Why would someone bother to do that? It was like they'd intentionally tried to create as much chaos as possible.

And they'd been here in the short window of time between when Avery and I left and now. Goosebumps prickled my skin. What if Avery and I had still been here when this person broke in? Or had they intentionally waited for us to leave?

I tugged my mind back. Now wasn't the time to think about that. I couldn't let myself be scared. Detective MacIntosh called me here for a reason. My fear wouldn't help him catch who did this.

I turned to ask him if we could go into the back kennel so I could look around there. He was staring at me, a slight smile on his lips.

I glanced down. I'd forgotten to zip up the jacket I'd grabbed to fend off the middle-of-the-night chill. My navy-blue pajamas with the red trim and Winnie the Pooh's face big and bold and yellow across the front were on full display.

I wrapped the jacket closed around me. "I've been here once tonight already. I didn't have the energy to change."

He grinned, transforming like magic from average-looking to handsome. "Or to brush your hair."

He reached out a hand as if he were going to touch

one of my loose curly-waves. He froze and dropped his hand back to his side.

His smile vanished. "I'll walk you through the office and kennel area."

My throat was strangely dry. I swallowed hard twice, gave up, and nodded instead of trying to speak. I probably should have said something snarky to him about the hair comment, but nothing came to mind. He hadn't seemed to mean it as an insult. Had anyone else looked at my hair that way, I would have assumed they thought it was pretty.

We walked through the manager's office, the staff room, and back into the kennel area.

The kennel area was in as much chaos as the front. Food lay scattered across the floor, and the drawers where we stored the medications had all been pulled open. Something about it struck me as strange. I tilted my head to one side and squinted as if the answer would appear like the images that popped out of those retro magic eye pictures. Maybe it was that *all* the drawers were pulled out. Because unless you started from the bottom and worked your way up, which seemed unnatural, you wouldn't be able to get into the bottom drawers with the top drawers still open. The top drawers would block them. You'd have to close the top drawers, at least partially, to access the ones below.

"Can I check the medications?"

He nodded and handed me a pair of gloves. "We've already photographed the way they were and finger-printed them."

I went through each drawer, mentally cataloging everything that was there without moving anything. "I don't think they took any medication. I think they just opened these drawers to throw us off of whatever they really wanted."

"That was my thinking, too, but I needed you to confirm that none of the medications were taken before I could be sure." He sounded almost impressed that I'd figured it out. "My suspicion is they were after something in your files."

Our files were primarily animal records and adoption contracts. The shelter did have some financial paperwork here too, though only the most recent months. Judith sent everything to their accountant quarterly. What could possibly be of use to an intruder? Maybe the bank account numbers? Judith would want to alert the bank to put a watch on their accounts for unusual activity for the next few months.

"Judith will have to go through the papers to figure out what might be missing. I'm not familiar enough with the management of the shelter to sort it out."

I headed down the aisles, making sure each animal was still there. The spilled food crunched under my feet. What a waste. "Do you think this break-in is connected to what happened to Bob?"

Detective MacIntosh walked beside me. "Right now, my working theory is that the person who shot Bob came back for whatever they were trying to get when they shot him. Maybe they expected the shelter to be empty when they showed up early this morning, and they shot Bob in a panic."

We came to the last kennel. Everyone was accounted for. My lungs let out the air I'd been unconsciously holding in. The animals were here and everyone looked okay. Everything else was replaceable.

I headed back the way we'd come. A tightness built in my chest and spread so my lungs didn't have room to drag in enough air. There was one other possibility. "Unless this was to cover up the real reason they came. If Bob was their target, if they were after him, coming back to toss the shelter after you released the scene would have been a great way to cover up their real motive."

Detective MacIntosh's face was solemn. "I'm considering that too. For now, I'm going to place an officer here to watch the shelter for the safety of the animals and another at the hospital to guard Bob. If this was about him, I want to be sure the perpetrator can't return to finish the job."

7

I set the final kitten down in the kitty play room. He zoomed away and launched himself onto one of his litter mates, setting off a chain reaction of running and tumbling and acrobatic leaps. "I think this is my favorite room."

Judith looked up from the oversized stack of papers in front of her. "Mine, too."

Her attention slid back to the papers. Sorting the paperwork into order and identifying anything that was missing was a bigger job than either of us had realized. Even more so now that Bob was in the hospital and another of the shelter's employees had quit out of fear. I was officially working on Saturdays for the foreseeable future.

The door chimed, and a middle-aged man walked in. He had a sturdy build, broad nose, hazel eyes, and mostly gray hair. Something about him looked familiar, as if I should know him. How long would I need to be back in

Arbor before that stopped happening? So many people I encountered were ones I'd known before I left for veterinary college, but they'd aged enough in my time away that they weren't instantly recognizable anymore.

I smiled at the man and moved away from the large window into the kitty play room. "How can I help you?"

"I have a few questions about adopting an animal." His voice was deep, with a hint of an undefined accent like people sometimes got when they lived abroad as a child.

The chime over the door sounded again. Crystal Rawlings' tall form filled the doorway. I glanced around the man I was talking to. She'd come without Gerald. I thought they were conjoined with how infrequently I saw them apart.

"You and Gerald finally going to adopt a brother or sister for Jasper," Judith called out. "Getting him a friend should help with his escape-artist ways."

I grinned even though I should have been paying attention to the man in front of me. Jasper was the first—and hopefully last—animal I'd treated on my dining room table when I first returned to Arbor, before I got the job at the vet clinic. I held a fond place in my heart for the little Basset Hound.

"I wish I was here to bring home another dog. I'm still working on Gerald. I'm here on council business." Crystal grimaced. "Sort of. Unofficially."

Sort of. Unofficially. That didn't sound good. Crystal was newly elected to the town council. After the incident where our last mayor turned out to be a murderer, the council decided to run a new round of elections. Some councilors decided not to run for re-election, like Keith, while others lost their seats. Over half the council was new. Whether the changes were for the better or not was still to be seen.

The man in front of me cleared his throat in an excuse-me-I'm-waiting kind of way.

I snapped my attention back to him. "Sorry about that. I'm happy to answer whatever questions you have."

"What do animals you adopt out receive?" His tone was formal, and the gaze he leveled at me said he was wondering how I'd gotten this job when I couldn't pay attention for more than two seconds.

My mouth dried out. I had to fix this. Fall meant we were overflowing with kittens. Even though they were safe, warm, and fed here, no kitten should have to grow up in the shelter. We couldn't replicate the kind of love and attention they'd get in a permanent home. The sense of safety and belonging that came with a family.

Offending a prospective adopter was the last thing I should be doing just to satisfy my curiosity.

I smiled brightly at him. "All our dogs and cats come spayed or neutered, dewormed, microchipped, and with their first set of shots."

In my peripheral vision, Crystal leaned on the large horseshoe-shaped desk that separated the area where Judith sat from the rest of the reception area. "You and Zoe helped save Jasper when he got that deep cut in his side, and I thought I owed it to you if I could return the favor somehow."

A scrabbling sensation took hold of my chest. That sounded ominous. Why couldn't she have come in a few minutes earlier so I could have been part of the conversation?

The man in front of me glanced over at Crystal as if he could tell I wasn't giving him my full attention. Judith would fill me in after. Patience was a virtue I needed to develop. This would be practice.

I made eye contact with the man. "Are you interested in a dog or a cat?"

"What about supplies." A hint of a British accent maybe. Or Australian? "Do you send them home with any of what they'll need, such as a bag of food."

"Each pet does go home with a bag of the food they've been eating while here. New owners need to supply collars, litter, all the rest."

He wandered over to the window of the kitty play room. Which put us farther away from Judith and Crystal. Only a few words filtered over to me. *Shelter. Attack.*

Crystal hadn't struck me as a busy-body the few times I'd talked with her, but we'd only interacted a handful of times. Maybe she was using her councilor position to learn what happened with Bob. That would be very unofficial business.

Do not listen to Judith's conversation. Pay attention to your own.

The man watched the kittens, his eyes shifting from side to side but his head still. He reminded me of a little boy who'd been reprimanded a lot as a child for fidgeting.

A small smile eased the lines in his face. "Do you allow fostering of animals, too?"

Ahh, this was a first pet. That's why he seemed a little uncomfortable. People who'd grown up in a home where they were constantly told pets were too much work were often hesitant their first time around. I always wanted to shake parents who taught kids that animals "took too much time." Pets didn't take any more time than playing a sport or video games or binge watching the latest show on TV, and those TV or video game characters couldn't love you back. "We're always looking for good foster homes. It's better for the cats and dogs, especially the young ones, if they can be in a home environment."

And most of the time people like this who came in only planning to foster because they weren't sure about pet ownership ended up keeping the animal they took in. Once you had a kitten fall asleep draped across your lap in the ultimate expression of trust, there was no going back. The long-time, repeat foster homes were generally the ones who were already experienced pet owners and were doing it as a service.

One of the kittens leaped into the air backwards over two others. The man's smile grew. "What do foster homes get for supplies?"

First time pet owner and maybe with a tight budget? Fostering would definitely be the best choice for him in that case. Though his clothes didn't strike me as someone on a tight budget. His shoes had tassels on them, and he wore a gold watch on his wrist. Maybe he was just a scrooge. Or maybe he was taught as a kid that pets were too expensive. Though the families who said that also usually ate out a lot or spent unnecessarily in other ways, so I called bull on that excuse as well. "We supply all food and medication for animals in foster care."

A small gasp came from Judith's direction. I glanced over. She had a hand over her mouth and the crumpled look on her face that said she was trying not to cry. Gah! I knew I should have been part of that conversation.

I motioned toward the kittens. "You're welcome to go in and meet them if you'd like. I'll be right back."

I hurried over to Judith and Crystal. "What's going on?"

Judith lowered her hand. "They're…" She swallowed hard and shook her head. She blinked rapidly, as if saying the words would also bring tears.

"It's not official." Crystal reached over the desk and squeezed Judith's hand. "I wanted you to know before anything turns official so you had time to fight it."

I could not yell at Crystal to spit it out. Not with a client in the building. I clenched my hands into fists. "What's not official?"

Crystal shifted to face me. I took a step back so I wouldn't need to tilt my head back to look at her. I always forgot how tall she was.

"You know I love animals, so I'm against it," she said. "But with the pit bull incident a few months ago, and the threats, and now Bob's attack and the break-in last week, there's talk of closing the shelter."

The only thing I could think was *no*. No, no, no, no, no.

I turned to Judith. "Can they even do that?"

Judith visibly swallowed. "Sort of. They can take our contract away. We're a charitable organization, and we bid for the contract to run the shelter. If they take away our contract, the shelter goes back under the control of the county."

My heart beat hard and fast in my chest, and my lungs couldn't seem to get enough air in around it. I rounded on Crystal. "Do you know what happens when a shelter goes from a Target Zero shelter, where the only animals who are euthanized are the ones too sick to save or too aggressive to rehabilitate, into a kill shelter? Perfectly beautiful, healthy, adoptable animals die. Innocent kittens." My throat closed, and I pointed toward the kitty play area. The man I'd been talking to before hadn't gone in, but he was still watching the kittens through the glass. He glanced back over his shoulder. I sucked in a breath and tried to lower my voice. "The shelter staff is completely innocent in everything that happened. All they've ever done is their job."

My voice ratcheted up in volume as soon as I'd started speaking again. Maybe there were times when yelling was necessary. This really felt like one of them.

Crystal held out her hands in a pleading way. "I know."

"They run microchip clinics and offer spay-neuter vouchers. They save thousands of animals every year."

"Zoe?" Judith said softly.

There was that use of my name as a question again.

The last time Judith used my name as a question, Orion had chewed up my cell phone.

"Yes?" The word came out more forcefully than I intended.

Judith cast a meaningful look in Crystal's direction. "You're shooting the messenger."

The fire in my chest snuffed out, and my shoulders drooped. She was right. "I'm sorry. I know you said you're on our side."

The chime over the door sounded, but instead of someone else coming in, it was the man leaving. Great. I'd probably frightened him away. No one wanted to deal with the crazy screaming lady.

Crystal grabbed my hand. "I'm fighting it, and so are a lot of others. So far we're still a majority. And this town loves animals, and I think if it ever did go to a vote, a lot of people would put pressure on their members of council to keep the shelter as is. I didn't want to worry you. It's just that if there was anything you could do to show the shelter was the victim of events and not a guilty party, you might want to do it."

Judith and I both thanked Crystal, though my voice sounded lackluster even to me. She blew us a kiss and left.

"Not a guilty party." I rounded the break in the horse-shoe-shaped desk and sank into the other chair next to Judith. "Basically, she wants us to somehow show that the shelter didn't instigate this? Or wasn't responsible? What does that even mean? You didn't do anything wrong with Tim Gilpin and his pit bulls. You were following the law.

The town council banned specific breeds in the first place."

Granted, Sebastian had ended up dead, but that had nothing to do with the shelter. The former mayor had a vendetta spurred on by a trauma in her childhood.

Judith propped her head in her hands. "I think the idea is that we could have handled that situation better somehow so that it didn't blow up the way it did. From what Crystal was telling me before you came over, some of the councilors think our charity isn't managing the shelter well. They think we must have done something again that's caused someone to come in and shoot Bob and toss everything around in retribution."

In other words, the council didn't care that they were blaming the victims. For them to leave the shelter alone, it wasn't enough for the shelter staff to not be at fault. "So we need to prove that Bob's attack had nothing to do with the shelter."

"No." Judith drew the word out. "I don't think that's what that means if you're thinking about investigating Bob's attack yourself. Last time you tried to figure out a murder, the killer tried to kill you."

Fair point. "I won't follow anyone into the woods again by myself. I do learn from my mistakes."

Judith pinched the pressure point at the bridge of her nose. "I'm not going to be able to stop you, am I? No matter what I say?"

"Nope."

Judith tugged her pile of papers closer and hugged it

to her chest. "For the record, I think you should leave the investigating to the police."

I examined her face. The tight set to her jaw, and her eyebrows pulled down slightly in the center. Her worries written in every line.

I wrapped my arms around her, and she leaned her head into my shoulder. I got it. I did. When a string of bad things happened, the world suddenly felt unsafe, like everything you cared about would be yanked from your grip and there was nothing you could do about it. But I couldn't batten down the hatches and bubble wrap the valuables, as our grandma liked to say. Hiding and depending on someone else to fix a problem had never gotten me anywhere. I had to do everything in my power or I'd always wonder if I was the reason things didn't turn out the way I wanted them to. At least if I tried and failed, I'd know I'd done what I could.

"I promise I won't do anything stupid, but this is too important. You save too many lives to go down without a fight. And I'm good at finding things out. I'll leave the actual chasing down suspects thing to Detective MacIntosh. Besides, if this person came intending to shoot Bob, Bob won't be safe until the shooter is caught."

8

I paused with the eyeliner halfway to my eyelid. I wasn't nearly skilled enough with makeup to apply it while also talking to my parents on the phone. Maybe I should just go without eyeliner. It wasn't like Keith hadn't seen me completely makeup-less before. Bare-faced was my natural state, and the bowling alley would be dim anyway.

"Is Judith home yet?" my dad asked. "Because there's something I wanted to talk to you about privately."

That sounded ominous. The only private conversation that happened when I was growing up were disciplinary ones. Mom and Dad had a policy about not reprimanding Judith or me in public, and that included in front of each other. Their theory was that correction given privately would cause less defensiveness.

But what could I have possibly done as an adult to merit a private conversation? I'd been behaving myself lately. I hadn't even hurt anyone's feelings...that I knew of. "Judith's still at work." I couldn't keep the hesitation out of my voice.

My dad drew in a long breath. "We didn't want to upset her when she's already under so much stress. We wanted to talk to you first."

I set the eyeliner down. I definitely wasn't going to be able to draw a straight line now. Orion shifted at my feet and cocked his head, his tongue lolling out, as if he could sense the change in my mood.

I scratched behind his ear in the place large dogs always seemed to love. He let out a happy groan. The sound sucked some of the tension from my body. "She's doing okay actually. You'd be proud of her."

"We're proud of both of you," Mom's voice cut in. "You're both strong in different ways. It's not that."

A chair creaked as if one of them were leaning closer to the phone.

"We just know that she's been friends with Bob longer than you have." My dad's voice was gentle despite how loud it still was. "And as parents, we sometimes have to be the ones to ask the hard questions. We've been alive longer than you girls, and we've seen more than you have. Sometimes people aren't who they appear to be."

My dad would know. Before he became a Christian, he was into all the same illegal things Tonya was. His change of heart was what broke them up because she didn't want to live a different life. I was three at the time. All I remembered about it was Tonya waking me up to leave in the middle of the night while my dad was at work. My dad fought for years to get custody of me, only succeeding when Tonya landed herself in prison on her first drug charge. Tonya had told me my dad didn't want me. One of her many lies that I didn't discover until later.

Not a surprise that Dad's life experience made him suspicious that Bob wasn't an innocent victim.

No wonder he hadn't wanted to ask Judith if he could avoid it.

I pulled the front of my hair back with a clip and secured it out of my face. That was fancier than a pony-tail or a braid at least. "Nothing less than an outright admission of wrongdoing will ever convince Judith of the guilt of someone she considers a friend."

"And we love that about her." My dad jumped in, as if he were worried I'd think they'd been criticizing Judith. "Her trusting nature and loyalty are beautiful qualities."

They were also two of her weaknesses. When we were ten, she hadn't ever doubted the boy who kept asking her for her lunch money only on pizza day, claiming he didn't have anything to eat. The third time it happened, I spotted the pattern and forced him to admit the truth.

Which was why my parents brought this to me. The skeptical one. The one with trust issues.

The one who'd be willing to consider what they were saying and take precautions if need be.

"We don't want to cast doubt on Bob's character. He always seemed like an honest man." Mom's words came out hurried, as if I'd been quiet longer than I realized and now she was worried about what I was thinking too. "We just want you girls to be safe. If he was doing something that resulted in the shooting—"

"No, I understand. It makes sense to wonder about what caused the shooting." Too much sense. Why hadn't I thought of it? Maybe I really was becoming more like Judith. Bob as an intended target made much more sense than a random shooter or someone with a vendetta against the shelter. And if he were the intended target, then there was a reason the shooter wanted him dead. "I'll make sure we're careful until the police catch the shooter."

I'd do more than that. A little poking around myself to see if any red flags popped up wouldn't be bad. Because if Bob had been lying to us about not knowing why someone wanted to shoot him, then I was going to keep Judith far, far away from him, whatever it took.

I picked my phone up off the desk and switched it off speaker. "I need to go. I'm supposed to meet Keith out front in a couple minutes."

"Tell him we say hello."

"I will."

I disconnected the call and dialed Judith's number. She answered, sounding tired.

Did misleading her count as lying? And if so, was it ever okay to lie to someone to protect them?

"I had an idea." I forced brightness into my voice. "I was wondering if you'd like Keith and I to take care of Bob's pets tonight so you could go straight to the hospital."

If I didn't find anything suspicious at Bob's house, she'd never need to know my motives weren't entirely pure.

9

I wiggled the key into the lock on Bob's front door. Judith warned me it would stick a little.

From the outside, his house was modest, and exactly what I would expect from an animal control officer's salary. He also drove a ten-year-old vehicle. Both of those had to be evidence that Bob wasn't into anything illegal.

Stop that, I admonished myself. *You need to stay objective.*

"Let me see the list again." Keith's hand reached over my shoulder. "That way we can divide and conquer and get to the restaurant at a reasonable time."

I passed him the list, and a little smile tugged at my lips. When I'd told him we needed to come here first before our date, he hadn't complained. He'd actually been happy to have a way to help Bob. How many men would do that, especially when it meant canceling our plans to go bowling in the city and staying in Arbor for dinner instead? Not many.

The lock released, and I pushed the door open. "Do you want the cats or the bunnies?"

Keith was still reading the list of instructions Bob had written out. "Cats. I'm pretty sure I can figure out how to clean litter boxes and fill food dishes, but I've never taken care of a rabbit before."

I left Keith with the list and headed off to find the sunroom where Bob's two rabbits had their pen. The living room said *I live within my means* as much as the outside of the house had. A small TV was mounted on the wall, and the furniture had a lived-in look to it—the edges of the couch and recliner a little frayed where multiple kittens had sharpened their tiny claws before learning to use their scratching posts.

A seed of hope unfurled in my chest. The shelter being targeted would be a bad thing, but I'd rather that be the case than that Bob wasn't who we thought he was. So far Bob looked like exactly who he seemed to be.

I glanced back over my shoulder. Keith headed down the stairs into the basement where Bob's instruction list said two litter boxes would be. That should give me time to check for drugs without making Keith suspicious.

An internet search had given me a list of places that drug addicts were most likely to hide their stash. I stopped at the main floor powder room and peeked inside the toilet tank. No baggie of drugs. I mentally crossed that spot off my list.

I let the rabbits out of their pen for some free time. The black-and-white dwarf rabbit took off running, leaping into the air and kicking out her back legs, just the way Bob said she would. The English lop with her giant, floppy ears followed more sedately behind.

Bob's computer sat on a desk in the corner. Odds were I wouldn't be able to get past the password, but it was worth a try.

I moved the mouse, and it came to life without a password. What kind of person didn't even have a password on their computer? An honest one with nothing to hide, hopefully.

The files on his desktop were pretty minimal. An instruction manual for the carpet cleaner sitting in the other corner. A couple legally purchased digital downloads of movies I'd heard about but hadn't seen.

His internet search history was equally mundane. He watched funny cat videos and read ESPN. He'd been looking at the bestseller lists for historical novels. He had an account with the same ancestry company I'd used as my attempt to find Harper, right after my grandfather's estate lawyer told me I had a half-sister I hadn't known about. Hopefully Bob had more luck than I had locating relatives. Three months of searching by the lawyer hadn't turned up any more leads on Harper than my DNA cheek swab had.

That was something I couldn't continue to put off talking to my parents about. The lawyer said any information they could add might help us locate her. But asking them questions about Harper meant talking about Tonya. It was easier to pretend Tonya didn't exist. If I didn't talk about her, I could almost imagine I was Camille's blood daughter and Judith was my genetic sister, and we'd never known anything other than a happy child-hood together.

I sighed. Except that fantasy wasn't real, and Bob's shooting proved that you never knew what a day might bring. I'd only end up hating myself if I kept putting off asking them about her and that delay somehow cost me my chance to know her. Like if she passed away before we ever met.

The next phone call with my parents would be the one where I asked them. In the meantime, I'd do everything I could to set their minds at ease about Bob.

I checked the remaining few files on Bob's computer. Nothing suspicious or out of the ordinary in any of them. No pornography hidden under a different file name. No files full of strange strings of letters and numbers that might be code for something illegal.

I pulled open the desk drawer. Bob's tax files lay inside.

The muscles in my chest clenched. Judith wouldn't like this if she ever found out. She'd see it as a betrayal of privacy. But this was for her too. To both keep her job at the shelter safe and to make sure she was safe around a man who was one of her closest friends.

I skimmed the last five years of tax returns, all completed using a small local tax firm that I'd seen the signs for around town. His tax returns were straight forward. One source of income, right in line with what I knew the shelter paid, and very few deductions other than a small amount of medical and a generous sum for chari-table donations.

The crushing sensation in my chest eased slightly. Bob might be exactly what he seemed.

The bunnies had run off into the rest of the house. I'd come back later to clean their litter boxes and give them their fresh food, but first I'd sneak upstairs to Bob's room while Keith was still busy.

I hurried up the stairs. The full bath on the top floor didn't have drugs hidden in the toilet either, and the pills in the Tylenol bottle were actually Tylenol, stamped and everything. Underneath his mattress, in his shoes, and inside his alarm clock didn't turn up any drugs either.

"Zoe!" Keith's voice had a panicked edge to it. "The rabbits are loose, and I can't catch them."

I hurried to the top of the stairs. "I let them loose."

"With the cats?"

"Bob said they get along. All the cats were raised with rabbits."

"I'd still feel better if you were down here. I don't know how to tell play from prey."

I quickly cleaned the upstairs litter box in case Keith asked what I'd been doing up here and headed down. There wasn't much else I could look into while Keith was with me anyway.

There wasn't much else I could look into at all. Bob seemed to be exactly the man he appeared to be. Maybe the shelter really had been the target. Or something in the shelter's files?

When I came downstairs, Keith was in the kitchen, opening cans of cat food. Bob's five cats circled around his feet, letting out a chorus of mews. One even stretched up Keith's leg and reached for the can with his paw.

Warmth bubbled up inside me. This was what I hadn't been able to have with my tiny apartment in Lansing. There'd been a one pet limit, so Orion had been it. Things could be different now. I could adopt cats and maybe even a doggie brother or sister for Orion.

I got the carrots and lettuce out of the fridge for the rabbits. "I think Bob's living my dream life. Minus the being shot part."

Keith spooned food equally into five dishes. "I wouldn't envy anyone being shot at."

Something in his tone was almost longing though, as if he meant the opposite. Was he missing the military? He'd finished his contract and decided to retire after his last tour of duty ended, but that didn't mean he wasn't regretting the choice now. And his position as pastor of our church was only a temporary spot until my dad came back from his missionary work overseas. After that Keith could go back to being a military chaplain if he wanted.

We hadn't talked about what he'd do after my dad returned. Should we? Or was it too early in the relationship? Other than Sebastian, I hadn't dated anyone for this long. Were there rules about when to talk about certain things so you didn't come across as intense and needy?

Keith bent over to set the first two dishes down. "This many animals seems like a lot of work. And they'd make it difficult to travel."

My heart rate kicked up a little, like I'd been out for a run. Don't panic. Do not panic. There had to be some way we could work this out. Surely that's what Judith would tell me. She'd accused me of giving up on relationships post-Sebastian too easily. I wouldn't do that this time. But this was important, too. "They would. But I think it'd be worth the trade off."

There, my voice sounded casual yet confident, didn't it?

Keith placed two more dishes on the floor and made a non-committal sound. "A pet wasn't something I could have when I was deployed more months than I was State-side, so maybe I don't know what I'm missing. I did enjoy seeing other parts of the world, though, and I'd like to travel more in the future."

All the dishes were on the floor now, and Keith was surrounded by a sea of content cats. Surely he couldn't hear those happy slurping noises and not have it melt his heart.

He jutted his chin toward the dish of carrots and lettuce I'd put together. "I'll wait in the car while you finish up."

Then again, maybe he could. He'd taken care of everyone, but he hadn't seemed that interested in cuddling them or picking them up. I snapped a picture with my phone of them all eating and sent it to Judith for Bob, then I knelt down and pet each cat before taking the vegetables and fresh water back into the sunroom. The bunnies must have seen what I had because they followed behind me.

Bob couldn't be into something criminal. He just

couldn't be. Too few people in this world cared about animals the way he did.

I added pellets to the bunnies' dish, cleaned their pen, and closed them back up. I should head out to join Keith, but it wasn't that late, and he wouldn't know how long I needed to finish up. If I was quick, I could call Detective MacIntosh and ask him if they suspected Bob of anything nefarious. They'd have looked into parts of Bob's life that I couldn't.

I dialed his cell phone number. The phone rang twice.

"MacIntosh." He sounded distracted.

"It's…" I almost said *Zoe*, but the word stuck in my throat. Somehow that seemed overly personal. And after that uncomfortable hug I'd thrown at him a few months ago when he brought Orion back to me, I didn't want him getting the wrong idea. "Dr. Stephenson."

"Hello, Dr. Stephenson." Was that laughter in his voice? "How can I help you? Do you have a bunch of theories about one of my cases already? I bet I can guess which one."

If this wasn't so important, I'd hang up on Detective Smug. "Actually, I was hoping you could give me some information."

"You know I can't if it's related to an open case and not already public knowledge."

His uprightness would be annoying if it wasn't so frustratingly admirable. How could I explain this is a way that wouldn't make him lock down everything he knew? He certainly didn't owe me any favors that I could call in. If anything, I owed him a favor for helping me get Orion back when the previous mayor wanted to have him euthanized.

"I'm not looking for that kind of information. Not technically." My skin was threatening to burn off my face. Thank goodness he couldn't see me. This was practically groveling. Spit it out already, woman. "I was hoping you could tell me...do I need to be worried about Judith spending time with Bob? Is there any reason you might know of why that friendship wouldn't be safe?"

"Ah." He said it as if he read more into it than even I intended. "Well, what I can tell you is that I was concerned for the safety of both our mutual friends, and I dug into that avenue of inquiry myself. It appears that our friend was in the wrong place at the wrong time and hadn't done anything to bring his injuries on himself."

I slumped against the wall and grinned. There were enough people in the world who couldn't be trusted. It was comforting to know there was one who could.

A text notification pinged on my phone. *Almost done?* Keith wrote.

Coming, I texted back.

I thanked Detective MacIntosh and hung up. I jogged toward the front of the house.

If Bob hadn't brought the shooting on himself, then someone had to be targeting the shelter. Tonight, I'd focus on my date with Keith. I owed him that for changing our plans last minute.

Tomorrow I'd visit Bob at the hospital with Judith and see if the three of us could come up with any reason someone might want Arbor's animal shelter to close.

10

The doctors hadn't placed any restrictions on Bob's diet since he was in the hospital for a gunshot wound, not something like a heart attack, so Judith and I picked up Chinese food and brought it to the hospital.

Bob was pushing something with a gray tinge around in a bowl when we showed up. His expression clearly said he was wondering whether it was better to go hungry.

He held up a spoonful and dribbled it back into the bowl. "When I asked what it was, they told me 'soup.' I've been trying to decide if it's cream of broccoli or potato and bacon. It doesn't actually taste like either." He grimaced slightly. "It doesn't actually taste like much of anything."

I pulled the bag of Chinese from behind my back and wiggled it slightly. "Then you're going to love us even more than you already do."

Judith's face went red, and she busied herself settling

into the chair next to Bob's bed, taking extra time to make sure her crutches were securely tucked away.

Bob cleared his throat. "I knew there was a reason you two were my favorites." There was a weird crack in his voice.

Okay, what was going on here? They weren't a couple. Judith would have told me that. So I was probably reading things into their relationship that weren't there. Bob was ten to fifteen years older than us, after all. But did one of them have unrequited feelings for the other, and I'd accidentally stepped into it? That would explain why the atmosphere in the room suddenly felt as awkward as if one of us had stripped down to our underwear and was dancing on the bed.

I moved Bob's mystery soup over to the bedside table belonging to the empty bed next to him. "On the bright side of all this, at least Detective MacIntosh got you a room all to yourself. Imagine if you had a roommate who snored. Or sleep walked."

Bob chuckled, but it felt forced.

I laid the Chinese food out on the tray, listing each dish. Bob and Judith still weren't looking at each other by the end. This was going to be a fun meal.

I'd intended to sneakily lead into us brainstorming ideas for why someone might want to hurt the shelter, but maybe they'd jump at the opportunity now simply to break the tension.

I plopped the vegetarian dumplings close to Judith since they were her favorite. "So, I was talking to Detective MacIntosh."

Judith's gaze snapped up to my face. "Did you call him or did he call you?"

Why did that matter? "I called him."

Her lips turned down slightly at the corners, as if she were disappointed, but the red had faded from her cheeks. Not the trade-off I'd hoped for, but it was something. Was she really this opposed to me involving myself in the case at all? All I was doing was a little of my own research. It wasn't going to be like last time.

I laid out the last container. "Anyway, he sounded sure that the person who was behind all this was looking for information in the shelter's files or they have a vendetta against the shelter or something similar." No need to mention why I'd called him in the first place. "I don't think there's any way to know which of the papers the guy was after if it was about the information in your files, but I thought we could help by brainstorming reasons someone might want to hurt the shelter."

Judith's lips had formed into the same line our mom's mouth took on when we'd been kids and did something she'd explicitly told us not to do.

I held up a hand. "That's something he's going to ask us and the other employees about as a normal part of his investigation." I made sure to emphasize *his*. "I'm not going rogue here. But the longer this drags on, the less chance there is they'll catch whoever did this. We can help speed up their investigation by making a list for them."

Bob slowly chewed a mouthful of chow mien noodles. "I don't see how that could hurt."

Judith glanced at him, and the strain lines around her lips eased. "Okay. I guess that would be helpful for Ryan's investigation."

I pulled a pen and a notepad from my purse. "Has the shelter received any threats of any kind lately?"

"None." Judith finally pulled the container of dumplings to herself and popped the top open. "You know I would have told you if there had been."

True. A few months ago, when I'd come home to take care of Judith after she broke her leg in a car accident, we'd had a fight because she hadn't told me she'd personally received death threats. Those threats had turned out to be nothing, but we'd agreed not to lie to each other anymore.

When my grandfather's inheritance turned out to be enough that I could become a partner with Maeve in the vet clinic, I'd even found the courage to confess to Judith about what happened at my last job. She'd helped me figure out how to tell Maeve as well.

I stirred my vegetarian fried rice with a fork. I'd never been able to master chop sticks. "Can you think of anything that might have made someone angry at the shelter? Threats always seem like they're more posturing to me. The person who's going to act won't want everyone to know they're going to act."

Bob and Judith looked at each other, but both their expressions were blank. Their default was obviously to think the best of people. Neither of them would have made a good police officer.

I'd just have to come up with possible situations

myself. "Did you seize any animals for abuse or neglect or levy any fines?"

Bob started nodding before I finished my question. "No seizures lately, but I did have to fine an owner. He has three dogs. A husky mix and two labs if I'm remembering right. And he hadn't licensed any of them, even though dog tag renewals were due in the spring." He deftly looped noodles around his chop sticks and took another bite. "But the fine only came out to a few hundred bucks plus licensing fees. That seems like too little to shoot me over."

Judith flinched. Bob was definitely taking his shooting better than she was.

I set down my fork and picked my pen back up. "What was the man's name? I'll give it to Detective MacIntosh anyway."

Not a lie. I would give the name to Detective MacIntosh, but I'd look into it myself first. Detective MacIntosh had made it clear that he didn't want me throwing every idea that came into my head at him. If I did that, he wouldn't take me seriously when I had something important to bring to him.

"David Atwood," Bob said. "His phone number and address are in the shelter files if the detective needs them."

Hopefully he would. Hopefully Atwood would be who we were looking for, and this would all be over. But before I turned the information over to Detective MacIntosh, I'd see if Mr. Atwood had an alibi for the time of Bob's shooting. No one wanted to become the boy—or in my case, girl—who cried wolf.

Since the weather was beautiful, I told Judith I'd walk home so she could stay longer at the hospital. As soon as I was out the front doors, I dug my phone out from under the replacement foster-home paperwork for Avery that I needed to pass along to her. Somehow her paperwork had gotten lost in the chaos. Judith implied I might have forgotten to have her fill the forms out because it was the middle of the night, but I distinctly remembered completing the forms. Avery had asked if Star needed to sign with a paw print, and I hadn't been able to keep a straight face when I told her animals couldn't enter into legally binding agreements.

I made sure the sidewalk was clear in front of me so I wouldn't run into anyone or anything when I wasn't looking, opened the internet browser on my phone, and searched the online phone directory for David Atwood. Only one person matching that name in Arbor came up. No need to even search the shelter's files for his info.

I'd promised Judith I wouldn't do anything reckless, so I couldn't simply ask David Atwood where he'd been at the time Bob was shot. If he was the shooter, that'd be as good as painting a giant red dot on my chest and begging him to use me for target practice.

I had one other idea that might work and let me ask him about where he was when Bob was shot without him realizing what I was up to. The summer before I left for college, I worked in town hall, filing paperwork for the department that collected the fines for parking tickets and bylaw infractions. Arbor had a very specific bylaw on the books.

I dialed David Atwood's number. A man answered.

"Hello," I tried to make my voice sound nasally and a bit pretentious in my best impression of my boss from that summer. "Is this Mr. David Atwood?"

"That's me." His voice held the suspicion that everyone's did when they got a call from a number they didn't recognize.

"Well, Mr. Atwood." I added a sniff for good measure, but that was the extent of my acting skills. I'd never gotten a speaking role in the school plays when I was a kid. "I'm with Arbor's bylaw enforcement department, and I'm following up on a report that you didn't clean up after your dog around 7:30 in the morning, a week ago yesterday."

"I don't know who called you." His voice sounded tight, like he was clenching his jaw. "But I always pick up my dogs' crap. No one wants to step in that. I walk the same route every day. I'd be the one gettin' it on my boots if I didn't clean it up."

He seemed to care a lot more about my accusation than about the day and time I'd quoted. If he'd been guilty, wouldn't he have reacted more to hearing me ask about the day and time of Bob's shooting? Or even willingly admit to not picking up after his dog and taking the fine? A report that he'd been walking his dogs at that time would have been a great alibi for him.

He might not be involved in what happened at all.

That was all guessing, though. It didn't prove definitively whether he had an alibi or not. I had to see if I could get him to say something more. I switched my phone from one ear to the other. "Well, sir, the caller said the dog in question looked like a husky mix. Do you have a dog that fits that description?"

"Yeah." There was a scowl in his voice this time. "But so do a lot of other people."

"Do you have someone who can vouch that they saw you pick up after your dog on the morning in question?"

Please say no. Please say no. People killed for small amounts of money all the time. And for revenge. If this man had gone after Bob in a rage, then this could all be over before Bob left the hospital. If not, how long would Detective MacIntosh be able to keep officers outside Bob's house to keep him safe?

"I don't know how you can expect me to remember if someone saw me when I walk my dogs the same way every day." Dave Atwood sighed. "What was the day and time again?"

I told him.

"A week ago Monday? Wasn't me they saw then. That's the morning I went to the dentist before work. My wife would've walked the dogs that morning, so if someone reported a man, it wasn't our dogs."

His tone was jubilant, almost to the point of

reminding me of a little kid singing out a mocking na-na-na-na-na-na.

But no dentist that I knew of opened before nine in the morning. He might be lying to cover up where he'd really been. "And the name of your dentist is what, sir? We'll need to check that you did, in fact, have an appointment at that time."

"Dr. Parr. His office is on 11ᵗʰ Street."

I knew exactly where Dr. Parr's office was. He was my dentist before I went off to school. And his office didn't do early morning appointments. "Thank you, sir. You have a nice—"

He hung up before I could finish.

Would this be enough to take to Detective MacIntosh? Problem was, if I called him with it, and it turned out I was wrong about Dr. Parr's office, I'd lose what little credibility I had left.

But if I called Dr. Parr's office, I was taking another risk of someone figuring out that I wasn't who I was claiming to be. It wasn't like I could hide my phone number from caller display.

My palms turned slick, and I wiped them on my shorts. I'd done far scarier things than this. Besides, what could they really do to me if they figured out I was calling under false pretenses—hang up on me? Call me on it? That'd be embarrassing but not fatal.

I pulled up the number for Dr. Parr's office. Would they still be open or would I have to wait until tomorrow?

The phone rang. And rang. Did I leave a voicemail?

"Family Dental. This is Kirsten. How can I help you?"

I jumped and almost dropped my phone. "Hi. Yes. Umm, I was wondering if you ever have early morning appointments for people who need to come in before work."

"We do." Kirsten's voice carried the upbeat, overly chipper tone that only dental receptionists seemed to be able to manage by the end of a long day. "We just started offering early morning and evening appointments, starting at 7:00 am and going until 7 pm on Mondays and Tuesdays. Would you like to book one?"

"Actually, I'm calling because I think my husband is due for a cleaning and check-up, and he hates taking time off work to go. Would you be able to tell me when his last appointment was?"

"Sure thing. What's your husband's name?"

"David Atwood."

He had said he had a wife. Hopefully the receptionist wasn't friends with her or something. That'd be a dead giveaway that I wasn't who I said I was.

"Let me see…" Typing noises came from her end of the line. "It looks like your husband was just in last Monday. He did take one of the early morning appointments, though, so you're right about that."

And there went that idea. David Atwood couldn't have had anything to do with Bob's shooting. He'd been at the dentist at the time. We were back to no leads.

I faked a laugh. "I guess great minds think alike."

I disconnected the call and shoved the phone back in

my purse. Neither Bob nor Judith had been able to think of anyone else who would have been angry at the shelter. After he'd given me David Atwood's name, I'd even asked Bob if he could think of anyone personally who might have wanted to hurt him, but he couldn't. And the glare Judith gave me for asking had ensured I wouldn't be asking again. Our parents had been right that she wasn't able to be objective right now.

I turned onto our street and stopped dead in my tracks. An ambulance and four police cars, all with lights flashing, filled the street. My heart lurched in my chest, then kicked up so high and fast the pulse thudded in my neck and ears and filled my head with a low drone.

They weren't just on our street. They were in front of our house. Or Keith's.

11

_____

I sprinted down the street. My purse slammed against my side and back with each stride. My heart beat even harder against my ribs.

It couldn't be our house. It couldn't. Judith should still be safe at the hospital. She'd been planning to stay after I left and play cards with Bob. Hadn't she? Please God, let her still be at the hospital.

Keith's house, then? Was it Keith's house?

My chest was so tight I could barely get the air I needed to run. The road seemed to move under my feet.

I'd talked to him on my way to the hospital. He'd been fine. He'd felt fine. Had he slipped down the stairs? This made no sense.

I pushed my legs harder. Two more houses. One more house.

I skidded to a stop. The police cars weren't in front of Keith's house. They were parked in front of our house, but the house itself was peaceful except for Orion barking inside. Judith's car wasn't in the driveway, so she had to still be at the hospital with Bob. The police cars in front of our house were only spillover.

My vision expanded outward. The ambulance sat jammed against the curb in front of Avery's house.

Had she hurt herself doing yoga? Some of the poses she'd shown me looked like a person could throw out their back or dislocate their shoulder with one wrong move.

You know that wouldn't require this many police officers, a little voice of logic in my head said. *She could have taken herself to the ER if it was something small.*

Two paramedics rolled a stretcher out the front door and lifted it down the steps. Someone lay on the stretcher, but the blanket covered their face. Covered everything.

The paramedics set the stretcher down on the sidewalk. One wheel wobbled, refusing to roll straight.

Maybe it wasn't Avery. Anyone could be under that sheet. Maybe someone had come to visit her. Or… or…

Or nothing. You didn't call four police cars to a scene for someone who had a heart attack or fell from a ladder, either.

I sank down to our front lawn. Blood pound, pound, pounded in my head. My eyes ached as if they were going to burst with the pressure.

How could this be happening? First Bob, now Avery. Things like this weren't supposed to happen in small towns. At least Bob had survived. But Avery…

Bile burned the back of my throat, and I forced my

mind away. Breathe in. Hold for four. Breathe out. Hold for four.

We'd never again sit around her table, eating flaxseed cookies and sipping chamomile tea and laughing. She'd never come running down her front steps, hand waving and beads flapping. She wouldn't be only a phone call away when I needed someone to help me with my deep breathing.

I should have been more patient with her the last time I spoke to her. I'd called her yesterday to ask how she was doing with Star, and she'd wanted to tell me about how she was learning to read the cat's past lives. And because there's no such thing as past lives, I hadn't wanted to waste time listening about the book she was reading to teach her how.

And now she was gone.

Tears spilled down my cheeks, hot and sticky, and I let them. Avery would have liked that. She'd always said holding in your emotions wasn't healthy. She'd had a theory that all diseases were caused by unexpressed emotions.

Detective MacIntosh stepped out the front door. His suit jacket and tie were straight, and neat, and wrinkle-free as usual, but there was that slight hunch to his shoulders that he only let sneak in when he was exhausted and thought no one was looking.

He glanced in my direction, then did a double-take.

He trudged down Avery's steps and across the lawn to me. He crossed his arms over his chest and looked down at me. The sun behind him threw his face into shadows.

A weird little hysterical laugh bubbled up in my throat. I stamped it down. "I'm not covered in blood this time."

"Small favors." His tone was so dry it could have blown away like dust in the wind. "I think you should go inside your house, though."

I wouldn't be able to see what was going on if I went inside, and that felt important for some reason. It wasn't. I couldn't even see anything relevant out here, but it felt like someone should witness and remember. "She's dead, isn't she?"

"We haven't notified her fam—"

I glared at him.

"Yes." His voice was soft. "She's dead."

"How?" Did I really want to know? Knowing had to be better than imagining all the ways she could have died.

Detective MacIntosh lowered himself to the ground across from me, even though he was sure to get dirt and grass on his suit. He sat cross-legged, mimicking my stance. Given his suit, tie, and dress shoes, he looked so out of place that I would have laughed if we weren't sitting next door to a crime scene.

"She was shot. It's impossible to say for sure since we couldn't find a casing or a bullet from Bob's shooting, but there's a chance the killer is the same person who shot Bob. The bullet that killed Avery went through without fracturing, just like in Bob's shooting, suggesting an older weapon again. We'll know more once ballistics analyzes the bullet."

Thoughts of all the organs that bullet could have gone

through to kill her swam into my mind, and my vision blurred at the edges.

Hold it together a little longer. You can break down later.

I shoved the images away. Right now, I had to focus and think. To try to understand this. Maybe this wasn't about the shelter after all. Avery had no connection to the shelter other than her new foster home status, and that was hardly enough to kill over. We had foster homes who'd been at it for years. One of them would have been a better target if someone wanted to keep hurting the shelter.

"Did they take anything?" A quiver entered my voice. I went through a quick grounding exercise, feeling the grass beneath my fingers, smelling the dirt and a whiff of Detective MacIntosh's outdoorsy scent. "Do you have any idea why someone would hurt her?"

"They didn't take anything, but they didn't have time. Your boyfriend"—he tilted his head toward Keith's house —"had just pulled into his driveway and heard the shots. He called 911 and went running over. He stopped to help Ms. Dunhill, and that unfortunately gave the killer time to get away."

I opened my mouth to defend Keith but stopped. Detective MacIntosh's tone hadn't been accusatory. He wasn't saying Keith did the wrong thing by checking on Avery instead of chasing after the killer. The killer had a gun, after all. If Keith had gone after him, he might be dead, too.

My skin went clammy. Keith could have been shot just for coming to Avery's aid. For all he knew, the shooter might have stayed to kill him rather than running. How many more people I knew and cared about would be hurt before the police found this person?

"Zoe?" Detective MacIntosh's voice had a note to it that suggested he might have already tried addressing me as *Dr. Stephenson* without result.

I forced myself to focus on him so that he'd see I was fine and not in shock. I didn't need another trip to the hospital. "Yes?" I added a hint of challenge.

His lips twitched the tiniest bit at the corners, then went still again. "I know we tend to butt heads some—"

I snorted and then clapped a hand over my mouth. Some? Try every time we came within sight of each other. "Sorry," I said around my fingers. "Go on. Sometimes I laugh inappropriately under stress."

He shook his head, but that lip twitch was back, fighting with the tension around his eyes. "I know you've been poking around, trying to figure out why someone might have shot Bob. But if the same person killed Avery, then we can't know what they'll do next. I'd like you to do me a favor and stay away from this investigation."

How did he know that I'd been looking into things? It wasn't like I'd been obvious about it. So he'd probably made a good guess because I'd asked him about whether any red flags popped up around Bob. He probably didn't know about my call to David Atwood or to Dr. Parr's office. I hadn't given either of them my name when I called.

I narrowed my eyes and dried my cheeks on my sleeve. Was he worried I'd hurt the investigation? I'd done a good job figuring out who killed Sebastian a few months ago. It'd been me, not him, who'd put the pieces together.

"I didn't impede your last murder investigation. I ended up helping." But my help had brought me into his orbit a lot. Maybe he was tired of having to talk to me so much. A blind person could see how much I annoyed him. "I'm not going to be a nuisance, showing up at your office and taking up your time like last time, if that's what you're worried about. I'll only bring you something solid."

He made a noise in his throat that was practically a growl and leaned forward. "I'm worried about *you*. This man has no problem killing people. I don't want you drawing his attention and making yourself a target."

An electric zing shot through my stomach. He was worried about *me*?

Stupid, stupid body. He would worry about anyone he thought was in danger. That was his job.

Even if he was worried about me personally, it would be because of what happened with the mayor a few months ago. He must think I was an idiot who would intentionally confront the killer if I figured out who he was. Not that his low opinion of me should surprise me. He'd made it clear what he thought of me the first time we'd met and he hadn't believed the blood on my shirt came from a dog rather than Sebastian Clunes. And then later when he implied I was a good suspect because my biological mother was in prison for murder.

We weren't friends. We weren't anything to each

other. If I wasn't breaking the law, he had no right to order me around.

"I'm not going to do anything public like last time, and I won't put myself in any dangerous situations. I already promised Judith that." My voice rose with every sentence. "But I can't promise you that I won't think about this case and try to figure out if there's a connection between Bob and Avery that's not obvious. Because I have to. Two people I care about have already been hurt. My sister could have shown up a minute earlier at the shelter and been shot like Bob, and my boyfriend ran straight into a danger today. I'm already involved, and I'm not stupid."

"I don't think you're stupid." He pressed his hands hard into his knees. "Far from it."

Why did he have to be so hard to read? Was he mocking me? Like the way some people gave the back-handed *You're too smart for that* compliment.

Didn't matter.

I shoved to my feet. "Have an officer drop Avery's cat at my house as soon as it's convenient. She's a foster, and I need to make sure she's taken care of."

I stalked into my house before he could stop me. I closed the door and thumped my head back against it. The flames burning through my veins fizzled out.

Why had I lost my temper and stormed away? I could have simply thanked him for his concern and done what I wanted anyway. He hadn't done anything wrong. It wasn't his fault someone was attacking my friends. His only crime was worrying about me.

But he didn't keep them safe, either, a nasty little voice whispered in my head. *Isn't that what the police are supposed to do? Keep people safe?*

I groaned. That was absolutely not fair of me. Detective MacIntosh had no reason to think someone would want to hurt Bob or Avery. He certainly couldn't have predicted that Keith would run toward gunshots rather than staying put. Technically, if I was going to be annoyed with anyone, it should be with Keith for putting his life in jeopardy, shouldn't it?

But I wasn't. Because I would have probably done the same thing without thinking about the potential consequences. Because if I were the one in danger, I'd want someone to run toward me rather than hanging back where it was safe.

Which was all I really wanted to do now. Why couldn't Detective MacIntosh see that? All I wanted was to contribute in any way I could to protect the people I cared about. My safety didn't matter if I lost everyone who mattered to me.

I had to figure out who this killer was before they hurt anyone else. What Detective MacIntosh thought about it didn't matter. *Shouldn't* matter, at least.

In the meantime, I was going to go next door and hug Keith, and then I'd head to the hospital and break the news to Judith before she heard about it from someone else.

12

J udith hobbled into the kitchen the next morning, her phone held out in front of her. Her eyes were puffy and red. I probably didn't look much better. We'd fallen asleep, curled up on the couch together, like we hadn't done since we were kids. Thankfully, my first appointment of the morning wasn't until 9:30, so I had some time for a slower start.

Judith was still holding her phone out toward me as if there were something on the screen she wanted me to see. "Ryan texted to say there wasn't any blood or other evidence on Star, so someone will be dropping her off soon."

The catch in Judith's words made my eyes sting again.

She tucked her phone away. "Why are they bringing her here instead of back to the shelter?"

In the clarity that always seemed to return after I'd gotten some rest, it seemed a bit silly. "I couldn't stand the thought of her being shuffled back to the shelter like she wasn't wanted. I'd rather we foster her until she finds her forever home."

The doorbell rang "Joyful, Joyful We Adore Thee," a holdover from when our parents lived here. I jogged off to answer it.

A middle-aged police officer with a mustache and a put-upon expression stood at the door, a cat carrier in one hand and the litter box and bag of food I'd given Avery at his feet. I shouldn't have been so grumpy about giving Avery that litter box. It was a small thing. I should have done it with a gracious heart.

I took everything from the officer, put the food in the laundry room where we kept the other animal food, and carried the litter box straight to the second-floor bathroom. I'd give her a bed in there, and it could be home base while I slowly introduced her to Orion. We already had dishes and cat food in the linen closet from the pregnant stray we'd cared for last month until she had her kittens and a long-term foster home opened up for the little family.

I came back down for Star.

Judith stood by the now-closed door, peering out the window. "Ryan didn't bring her back himself? That's strange."

Not strange at all, considering the way I'd treated him yesterday. "He's a detective. He's probably busy. He has Bob's shooting and Avery's murder to investigate now. It makes sense for a regular officer to bring her."

Judith gave me a sidelong look, like she was thinking about saying something more. Instead, she tucked her crutches back against her sides. "I've got to get going for work. Are you still planning on calling Mom and Dad this morning about Harper?"

I nodded. Only regrets could come from continuing to put off this conversation. Avery's death made that clearer than ever. No more waiting for our regular Monday phone call with Mom and Dad to ask the questions I needed answered. No more waiting for my grandpa's estate lawyer to find a lead. If that hadn't happened in the past three months, it was never going to.

Besides, Detective MacIntosh wouldn't get crotchety at me for trying to find Harper the way he clearly would if I continued trying to find the person who shot Bob and Avery.

Judith hugged me, scratched Orion behind the ear, and headed out.

I took Star upstairs to the bathroom and sat on the floor with her. Her purr filled the room, and she head-bumped my hand every time I stopped petting her. Maybe we'd skip the foster part and adopt her instead. I'd talk to Judith later.

I dialed our parents' number.

"Zoe?" Mom's voice was almost drowned out by the noise of children's voices and traffic in the background. "What's wrong?"

The word *nothing* sprang to my lips. I stopped it before it could escape. Lots of things were wrong. The desire to tell them about Avery clogged my throat. But if I started there, we'd never make it to Harper. They couldn't bring Avery back, and they hadn't known her. She'd moved into the house next door after they left on their missionary work. I could tell them about her later. I couldn't wait to talk to them about Harper. I might lose my nerve.

"I need to ask you and Dad some questions about Harper."

"Hang on one second."

Mom's voice became muffled, but I could still make out her saying my dad's name and then mine. The sounds on her end faded and then disappeared.

"We're both here now." My dad's voice was softer than my mom's had been, as if she'd put the phone on speaker and he was leaning in from a distance. "What's happened with Harper?"

"Grandpa's lawyer still can't find her." It was like the barricade I'd put in place to keep it all inside clattered down around me in an avalanche of words. "The lawyer keeps apologizing for not being more thorough in getting our information from Grandpa. He made it sound like Harper and I would be together, so the lawyer assumed we had the same last name and address. Grandpa didn't tell her we didn't have the same father."

A small scuffling sound took place on the other end, as if the phone were being passed.

"You know you would have been together if we'd known about her, don't you?" Mom asked.

My throat thickened. "I know."

It wouldn't have mattered to either Mom or Dad that

neither of them were related to Harper by blood. The fact that I was would have been enough. They'd have adopted her and raised her as their own. But when I'd first learned about her existence, Dad had been as shocked as I was that I had a half-sister out in the world somewhere. All those years lost. I didn't even know how old she was. If she knew I existed, she might think I didn't want to find her because I hadn't made contact already.

"Did the lawyer search for a Harper Crawford? Maybe she has Tonya's last name because..." My mom let the sentence trail off and cleared her throat.

She didn't need to finish. Maybe she had Tonya's last name because Tonya didn't know who Harper's father was. With all the different men who were in and out of our lives after Tonya left my dad, it wouldn't have surprised me. But my mom was too kind to say any of that. She never wanted to sound like she was criticizing my biological mother even though Tonya would have deserved it.

Star rammed her head against me again. I scooped her up, but she squirmed, wanting the freedom to be an interactive snuggler. I put her down and ran both hands over her instead. "She found a few Harper Crawfords, but none of them were the right one. Without more to go on, it's like searching for one particular grain of sand on a beach."

"So you want to try to narrow down when she might have been born?" My dad's words were slow, as if he were thinking it through as he spoke. "Are we assuming Harper wasn't conceived while Tonya was in prison?"

Ugg. Just when I thought the situation couldn't get more sordid. "Yeah, let's assume that for starters."

My dad made a *hmm*-ing noise. "Tonya's first conviction, the one where I finally got custody of you, she was out in a year. So if Harper was born after that and before her next conviction, that'd make her about eight or nine years younger than you."

Still a legal adult. Barely. Danica Dickerson, grandpa's estate lawyer, said an adult would be easier to locate than a minor.

"Then there was the drug charge. She got five years for that one, but I think she might have gotten out on early parole. Do you remember, Camille?"

My mom made a negative sound. I didn't remember, either. I'd been too busy making sure everyone knew I didn't want to see Tonya or hear from her. I made life miserable every year for weeks before the court-mandated annual visit.

"Either way," my dad said, "that'd put her in her teens now if she were born between when Tonya got out that second time and the murder conviction. Fourteen, fifteen, sixteen."

Tonya had been particularly evasive those years, even missing one of our yearly visits. In hindsight, maybe she hadn't wanted me to know about my sister. Which wouldn't surprise me. Tonya liked to manipulate others. She'd probably been waiting for the best time to use Harper as a bargaining chip against me to get something she wanted. Ending up with a 25-year prison sentence short-circuited whatever plans she'd been making. I might never know what they were.

I shuddered. I probably didn't want to know. I ran a hand over Star's fur. Who needed a grounding box when you had a cat?

"If she's a minor," Mom said, "maybe Child Protective Services could help you find her. If her biological father didn't take her, she could be in foster care or with an adoptive family."

That was a practical step. I could do that.

I glanced at the time on my phone. Still a half hour left before I needed to leave for work. "I'll call them now."

We ended our call. I dialed the number for CPS. A woman answered the phone.

"Hi. Yes." Jitters ran through my body. This was worse than being on a first date. "My name's Zoe Stephenson, and I'm trying to find my sister. I don't know if she's in foster care or if she's been adopted."

My voice shook. Why was I so nervous? It wasn't like I was meeting Harper right this second. But this made it feel like I was so close. If Harper were in their system, I might be able to see her within weeks.

"Sure thing, sweetie. Let's start with your sister's name."

The million-dollar question. "Harper. Our biological mother's name is Tonya Crawford, but I'm not sure what Harper's last name is."

"Okay." The woman drew the word out. "How long has it been since you and Harper were separated?"

I poured out the whole story. The woman was patient with me even when I needed to pause and wait for my voice to come back.

She blew out a breath. "I can see your file and when we stepped in there, but it doesn't list any siblings, full or half. That complicates things."

A knot clogged my throat, blocking my words. I swallowed once, twice. The knot in my throat eased. "I was hoping you'd be able to search using Tonya's name. Harper should come up that way, even if she has a different last name, shouldn't she?"

"I can search for Tonya Crawfords in our system, but that results in multiple matches across the country."

My heart beat so hard in my chest that it hurt, and I couldn't quite draw a full breath. A search through that many people would take time, but surely it was still possible. I mean, really, computers could run spaceships. They could analyze complex scientific data. Harper was in their files, so the computer should at least be able to spit out possible matches.

"I can narrow down her date of birth to a few years if that helps."

"No, sweetie. I'm sorry. Let me try to explain." She paused. "You and Harper aren't linked in our system, and we have multiple women, and even children, with the name Tonya Crawford. I can't give you any information about Harper or try to set up sibling visitation without proof that you're her sister, even if I could identify which child in our system is most likely to be your sister. Our files are confidential for the safety of our clients."

"What am I supposed to do if you won't tell me how to find her?" The words blurted out before I could stop them.

I sucked in a breath. Would that count as confrontational? Most government agencies had policies about not dealing with people who became combative.

"Please," I added quickly. "I don't know what else to do. I didn't even know she existed until a few months ago, and now I just want to get to know her."

"Is your biological mother still alive?"

A stuttering sensation filled my chest. "Yes."

"And are you able to contact her in a safe way?"

Safe? Physically safe, yes. Emotionally safe, never. "She's in prison. I know how to reach her, but we haven't had contact since I turned eighteen."

"Okay, well, if you can get her to tell you Harper's full name and date of birth, I can look for a match in the system. Then we can arrange a DNA test. Once we have those results, then you have rights as her sibling. Until then, I'm afraid there's nothing I can do for you."

I thanked her, but my voice sounded like it belonged to someone else.

The woman made it sound so simple. Just go ask Tonya.

Well, she didn't know Tonya. Nothing with Tonya was ever free or easy.

When I turned eighteen, I promised myself I'd never have to see Tonya again. I'd kept that promise, and I'd never regretted it. My dad kept trying to help me see that she was a broken, sad person, and that I should feel sorry for her.

And I did feel sorry for her, but I'd also wanted my life to be free of her.

Now I had to decide if finding Harper was worth seeing Tonya one more time.

13

A very's ghost stood at my door.

I sucked in a breath so fast I coughed. Not possible. Ghosts didn't exist.

I blinked, but the woman didn't disappear.

Maybe I'd fallen asleep on the couch when we got home, and this was a dream. With Bob's shooting, Avery's death, and the possibility of seeing Tonya again hanging over my head, I admittedly hadn't been sleeping well. I'd almost dozed off sitting up when Judith and I were having Saturday morning breakfast with Bob.

That was it. I must be asleep.

"Who is it?" Judith's voice came from behind me. She gasped, and one of her crutches hit the floor with a bang. "Avery?"

Avery's ghost held up her hands. The bangles on her arms clinked together. "Ellery. I'm so sorry. You look terrified. Avery and I were twins. Are twins. Were twins. I... I'm not sure how to say it now."

My vision cleared as if blinking away a film of water. There were little differences. Avery had preferred beads. Ellery had so many chunky bracelets on her arms I couldn't see much skin. Ellery was more tanned, as if she spent her time out of doors instead of in the yoga studio. Freckles peppered the bridge of her nose.

"We didn't know you were twins," I said, sounding stupid even to my own years. That was obvious by now.

Ellery motioned in the direction of Avery's house. "I'm here to pack up her things and decide what to do with the house, but I didn't bring enough boxes or packing tape." The look on her face was the one people got when they were a breath away from breaking down. "I didn't realize she had so much stuff."

I glanced back at Judith, and she nodded as if she knew exactly what I was going to say. "Do you want some help?"

Ellery slumped against the door frame. "Would you?"

Judith grabbed the tape, and I gathered up an armload of deconstructed boxes from the garage where we kept them until we had enough to take to the recycling depot.

Ellery had left the front door of Avery's house hanging open. She waved us in. "I've been living out of my RV for the last few years, visiting every mainland state. I didn't realize how much a person could accumulate when they settled down in one place."

I stopped in the doorway. The inside of Avery's house looked like it'd belched the contents of every drawer and cupboard out into the living room. There were forks next to bottles of essential oils, piles of paper draped with colorful scarves, and shampoo and conditioner bottles at the end of the coffee table. Ellery must have gone around the house, gathered everything she could carry, and brought it here.

If the three of us worked on it all day, we might make a dent. Good thing Maeve had offered to cover the animal shelter today with one of the other employees so Judith and I could have the day off.

"Umm…" Judith's eyes were round as an owl's in her head. "Let's start with clothes."

Ellery bobbed her head. "I have most of those over here."

She led us to the far corner, nearest the dining room, where clothes were piled up like leaves in fall. If I was a kid, I would have been tempted to leap into them. Where had Avery stored them all?

"Do you want to keep any to wear yourself?" Judith's voice was a squeak, as if she were feeling the same way I was.

"Good idea!" Ellery started pulling her blouse off.

I was pretty sure she wasn't wearing a bra underneath. I turned around. Judith joined me. Her shoulder shook slightly where it touched mine. I glared at her and pressed a finger to my lips. If she cracked up now, I certainly wasn't going to be able to keep a straight face.

"I don't know who would do this." Ellery's voice was muffled as if she were pulling another shirt on. "Everyone liked Avery. She was always the more likeable one. She wasn't nearly as flaky as me."

Judith stilled beside me. The smile that been fighting to break free from my lips died as well. How could I have forgotten, even for a second, why Ellery was here? What kind of horrible person was I that I could even think about laughing at a time like this? Though Avery would have probably told me that was irrational. *Laughter is better than medicine,* she used to say. *It'll heal anything.*

"Another one of our friends was shot, too," Judith said. "He survived, but he's in the hospital."

Questions burbled up to my lips. I hadn't done any investigating about Bob's shooting or Avery's death this week. Not since my conversation with Detective MacIntosh. Despite what I'd told him about needing to continue trying to find answers, every time I thought about it, I kept hearing him say he was worried about me.

But now a safe opportunity had fallen into my lap to see if there was a connection between Bob and Avery that we weren't aware of. Detective MacIntosh couldn't expect me to walk away from that.

"We're trying to figure out if there's any connection between them that the police might have missed." Talking to her without looking at her felt rude, but fabric was still swishing around back there.

Judith raised an eyebrow at me, probably in silent protest at my use of the plural *we*. But it did need to be a *we* right now. She knew Bob better than I did.

"That's a great idea," Ellery said. "You tell me about your other friend, and I'll compare it to Avery. We'll be like Veronica Mars or those *CSI* people or something. Are either of those still on TV? It's been a while since I had one."

Judith started talking, while I caught the pieces of clothing that Ellery didn't want to keep and packed them into a box to be donated.

They covered the easy stuff first. Bob was a Christian. Avery was New Age. Avery taught yoga. Bob didn't even have a gym membership. They were about the same age, but born in different states. Avery was vegan. Bob liked a thick steak.

"Avery told me she just got a cat. Did Bob have pets?" Ellery walked around in front of us, fully clothed again. "Why are you still staring at the wall? We should go sit in the kitchen. Avery made the best tea blends. I'm going to miss them. She never wrote any of her recipes down."

Ellery's voice shook slightly, as if the best way she could hold herself together was to focus on small, incidental things like the tea rather than that her sister was gone.

Avery's mountain of clothes had been winnowed down to two skirts and three blouses.

Ellery filled the old-fashioned kettle and set it on the stove to heat. "Our family is wealthy. Maybe this criminal is targeting people from rich families, thinking they'll have something valuable in their houses."

I glanced around the room. No one looking at Avery's house would think she had money. Half the kitchen cabinets and drawers hung open, revealing mismatched cups and plates she'd gotten from yard sales. She'd called it *reducing the waste from our consumerist society*. "Bob's solidly middle class, and he wasn't shot at his house."

Ellery held out an unlabeled baggie full of leaves for Judith to smell. Judith's face had an expression of terror on it. Avery's tea blends might not have been famous, but they were infamous. Sometimes they were delicious, and sometimes it would be better to drink fishy river water.

"His dad was rich, I think." Judith edged back from Ellery's offering. "His dad was some antique dealer before he died, but he wasn't a part of Bob's life growing up. Bob's never even met him or had any contact with that side of his family. His parents had a one-night stand, and Bob was the result."

Ellery sniffed the baggie she'd been offering to Judith and smiled a sad smile. "That's not a match then, either. We were raised by both parents, and we had everything we wanted."

She said it so matter-of-factly that I almost couldn't fault her for it. It didn't even sound like bragging. Why would someone who was given everything growing up toss it aside to live in her RV and drive around the country? Or, perhaps, that's why she had the freedom to do it. And why Avery had the freedom to work as a part-time yoga instructor. They didn't need to worry about how to pay their bills.

Not that traveling around the country was anything I'd want to do even if I could. The idea of shuffling from place to place reminded me too much of how Tonya moved us around. All I ever wanted was to stay someplace long enough to make friends and feel like I knew a place. To stay somewhere permanently so I didn't have to keep putting all my belongings into boxes and keep deciding what was valuable enough to take with us and what had to be left behind.

Ellery filled a tea ball with leaves and poured boiling water over it. "Have the police considered a serial killer?"

I'd already researched that option. Only one percent of all the murders in the U.S. were committed by serial killers. The odds that we had a serial killer in Arbor were almost too small to calculate considering how few murders we had. If this was a serial killer, we'd already be over our lifetime quota. Plus, a killer had to commit more than two crimes to earn the title.

"I don't think it's a serial killer. Serial killers generally have types, and we've spent the last hour establishing that Avery and Bob have basically nothing in common." A whiff of the tea reached me. Mold and dirt. My stomach turned. Judith might choke it down for Ellery's sake, but I wasn't going to. "We should probably get back to sorting through everything, don't you think?"

I backed toward the living room. Judith followed me as fast as her crutches would carry her. Ellery trailed us, still holding her cup of tea, as if she'd forgotten she was supposed to make two more cups.

We'd already finished the clothes, which were the easiest. Maybe we should do papers next. Most of those could be shredded.

I headed for the lime-green beanbag chair and plucked Avery's salt lamp off the pile of papers. Had she actually put it away when she brought Star home, or had she ignored all my instructions? I guess I'd never know now. And it didn't matter anymore.

I held up the lamp. "Stay or go?"

Ellery wrinkled her nose. "Keep if I keep the house. Go otherwise."

My estimate for how long this would take had definitely been too optimistic. Forget days. We might be looking at weeks at this rate. I set the salt lamp with a pile of earrings on the coffee table. A tax folder sat on the top of the pile of papers. That was something Ellery would need to keep whether she wanted to or not. At least until she'd filed Avery's final taxes.

I picked up the folder and froze. I knew this logo.

I held it up so Judith could see it. "Winger Accounting. This is the same company that does Bob's taxes."

She gave me a look that clearly said *And how do you know that?*

Her gaze focused on the folder, and the look evaporated. "That's the accountant who does the shelter's books too."

14

"Do you think Bob or Avery discovered their accountant was doing something shady?" Judith asked.

I flipped open Avery's tax folder. As Ellery had said, the bulk of Avery's income wasn't from her yoga instruction. She'd been living primarily off of investment income. "Maybe. They wouldn't have both figured it out, though, would they?"

Judith moved over to one of the beanbags and glanced down at it as if she intended to sit. Then she must have thought better of how hard it would be to get up again because she stayed standing. "Maybe one of them figured it out and asked the other about it because they knew they used the same accountant?"

Ellery sipped her tea, the tea ball still in it, her head swiveling back and forth between us as if we were a fascinating stage play. "Avery had a taste for married men. Maybe she was having an affair with this accountant and your friend Bob found out about it. Though, an accountant doesn't really seem like her type. She preferred men who liked the outdoors. Skydiving instructors. Base jumpers. Back-country skiers."

Those sounded to me like men who had a death wish, but to each their own. Ellery's theory was a viable one, regardless. If Mr. Winger turned out to be married. We had a lot of questions, and there was only one way I could see to get any answers.

I placed the tax folder into a box for Ellery, and wrote *Important Documents* on it in permanent marker. "I'm going to go talk to him."

Judith opened her mouth, but I held up a hand.

"I'll go to his office, during normal business hours. That way I'll be safe, just like I promised you."

Going to speak to the accountant wasn't the perfect solution. If he were the killer, I'd still be painting that target on my back that Detective MacIntosh had been so worried about.

But if I went to Detective MacIntosh and said *Bob, Avery, and the animal shelter all have the same accountant*, his response would likely be that most people in Arbor used that accounting office. Judith and I didn't, though, so this might not be a coincidence. It might mean something. When nothing else seemed to tie Bob and Avery together, we couldn't overlook the one thing that did.

***

I drove my car to work on Monday rather than walking despite the day possibly being one of the last beautiful moments of fall. According to Judith, the accountant's office was on the opposite side of town from the vet clinic, and they were only open for a half hour past when the vet clinic was. I needed to time things perfectly if I was going to get there before they closed.

I found it easily.

The office was longer than it was wide, with a hallway leading back into the depths. It smelled faintly of feet and an industrial-strength cleaner.

The reception desk was empty. A bell sat on it with a little sign propped up, saying, *Ring for Service*. I'd expected there to be other people here. Being alone with Mr. Winger didn't check off the *Stay Safe* box for this endeavor.

I glanced out the front windows. They were large and faced onto a busy street. As long as we stayed up here and I didn't go back into an office where no one could see us, I should be fine. Besides, it wasn't as if I were going to ask him directly if he'd murdered one person and tried to murder another.

I tapped a finger onto the bell. The pathetic clink it gave off didn't seem loud enough to alert anyone that I was there.

A man in his late fifties came out of one of the back offices. He wore a dull navy suit and thick tie I'd expect from an accountant, but his chin was cartoon-character broad, with a divot in the center.

I backed up a step so that I was close to the door. Despite what Detective MacIntosh might think, I didn't *want* to place myself into dangerous situations. "Are you Mr. Winger?"

He smiled, but it looked anemic compared to his jawline. "I am. How may I help you?"

You can help me by showing me whether you're a murderer or not. "I have a couple of friends who use your services—Bob Bremnes and Avery Dunhill."

Mr. Winger tilted his head. "You're friends with both of them? They're an odd pairing."

He hadn't twitched or flinched or looked away at the mention of their names. Nothing. He acted like he hadn't even heard of what happened to them. He'd used present tense for Avery.

Maybe he hadn't heard about her death. I thought rumors and news traveled fast around Arbor, but that might be because I was a member of a church and I worked at the vet clinic. Clients often wanted to make small talk while I conducted their pet's annual exam.

"I'm friends with both of them." I pasted a smile on my face. This would be so much easier if I could ask direct questions the way the police did. Then again, my advantage was that people wouldn't suspect me of digging for information about a crime the way they would the police. I pointed back at the sign hanging on the door with his hours. "Do you ever take appointments earlier?"

If he were here with a client the way David Atwood was with his dentist when Bob was shot, then that would cross him off the suspect list.

"Not as a regular practice."

Had a small edge entered his voice or had I imagined it? "That's too bad. Your hours overlap with the hours I work."

Mr. Winger moved around me and pointed to a slot next to the door that I hadn't noticed. "We have a drop slot for clients to leave paperwork for us during off hours."

That would be convenient to have if I was actually looking for an accountant. But it didn't help me at all with finding out if he might have killed Avery and shot Bob. "Bob was telling me how important it is to find an accountant with integrity."

He hadn't really told me that, but it seemed like something Bob would say if I asked him. So maybe that meant it wasn't an outright lie? Though, I'd already crossed that line a couple of times trying to figure out the truth. Was it getting too easy to justify? If I wasn't careful, would I be justifying lies for the "greater good" in my regular interactions, too?

Mr. Winger smoothed his hands down the front of his suit jacket and checked his buttons. The gesture made him look nervous. He might only be anxious for me to be gone so he could go home, but it was the first sign of unease he'd shown at all.

I'd have to face the ethics of what I was doing later. Right now, I had to stay the course or this trip would be wasted.

I blasted him with my best innocent smile. "I was hoping you could tell me what safeguards you have in place for your clients to make sure everything is done ethically. And what you would consider red flags about an accountant."

Mr. Winger glanced at the doorway. He moved over

to the reception desk. "Those are big questions, and I'd be happy to answer. How about we make an appointment for a free consultation?"

Something about those questions definitely made him uncomfortable. That wasn't enough to take to Detective MacIntosh, though. He wouldn't be convinced by *The man seemed nervous*. I could hear him now. *Most people get nervous when a stranger interrogates them. That doesn't make them guilty of a crime.*

The last thing I wanted to do was make an appointment. That would give him time to prepare answers. It'd also give him my name. "I can't come in during regular hours, remember."

The door behind me opened, letting in a rush of fresh air.

"Zoe?" Keith's voice said. An arm slid around my waist, and a kiss pressed to my temple. "This is a nice surprise. What are you doing here?"

I stiffened. Oh, crap. Keith would be furious over the truth. Maybe he didn't actually expect an answer.

Mr. Winger's face went a pasty gray, making him look like a sketch of a person rather than a live person. "This is your girlfriend? What did you tell her?"

Keith's hand tightened on my waist. The movement would have been imperceptible to anyone watching.

My face and hands went cold. What did Keith tell me? As if Keith knew of something Mr. Winger had done? Like shoot Bob and kill Avery?

Keith was a pastor, though, not a priest. A pastor didn't have the same confessional confidentiality thing. If someone told Keith they'd committed a crime, he'd have a legal obligation to tell the police. I'd once made assumptions about Keith and falsely accused him of lying to me. I knew him better now. He wouldn't cover for a murderer. But then what was going on?

Two red spots filled back into Mr. Winger's cheeks. "She came in here asking me questions about my integrity and trustworthiness. You must have told her."

"I didn't tell her anything. I'm sure this is a misunderstanding." Keith's arm dropped from my waist, and he angled toward me. "What are you doing here?

A lie rose up to my lips, ready to go. I was here because I thought my accountant might be doing something shady, and I wanted the advice of another professional in the same field.

Except that would slander my accountant. Who seemed like an honest man and had been doing my taxes since I got my first job. Even after I moved to the city.

And it'd be lying to Keith. I couldn't expect honestly from him if I didn't give it in return. Trust and honesty were essential to a relationship, and they had to go both ways. Bad enough I hadn't shared the entire truth of my past with him. I couldn't start hiding my present, too.

My mouth dried out as if I'd eaten too many Saltine crackers. "He files taxes for Bob, Avery, and the animal shelter. It was the only thing we could find that they had in common."

Keith sighed and scrubbed a hand over his hair. "I'm sorry about this, Ed. She doesn't know. But what she's thinking you've done is much worse. I recommend you tell her the truth. She won't tell anyone, and you won't have to worry about her bothering you anymore."

Bothering him? Like I was some sort of pesky child?

A pit opened up in the middle of my stomach and threatened to swallow my heart whole. That was probably how Keith saw my investigating. To him, I was a grown-up still wanting to play make-believe.

Mr. Winger fisted his hands and pressed them into the desk. "I don't know her. And right now, I'm not sure I can take your word for anything."

Keith stepped away from me, putting more space between us. Like I was tainting him by association. "Tell him why you're here."

An angry retort that I didn't appreciate being ordered around sprang to my lips. I bit it down. It was more important right now that I find out the truth. If I was looking at the wrong person, I didn't want to waste time or accidentally drag his name down by suggesting him to Detective MacIntosh.

"Someone shot Bob Bremnes and murdered Avery Dunhill." I kept my voice flat and factual. "The only connection between them seems to be that they used your tax preparation services."

"They're dead?" Mr. Winger's mouth drooped open. "And you think I killed them? I didn't even know about what happened until right this second."

Keith gave me a look that could have cracked granite. As if he thought there was no possible excuse for what I'd done.

He turned back to Mr. Winger. His expression softened. "I'm so sorry she came here, Ed. She won't come back. But I do think it's best if you tell her."

Mr. Winger cleared his throat. Cleared it again. He looked at me with eyes both angry and ashamed. "I attend AA meetings. My addiction doesn't affect my work anymore. I've been sober six months now."

That doesn't necessarily mean he didn't hurt Bob and kill Avery, a mischievous voice whispered in my head. He'd said it didn't affect his work *anymore.* That meant it had at one time. He could have made some major mistake on their taxes before he stopped drinking. Maybe they were talking about reporting him to whatever governing body licensed accountants.

"I drove him to an AA meeting the morning of Bob's attack," Keith said, as if my thoughts had been plastered on a billboard above my head. "I sat with him during the meeting. If you want an alibi for him, I'm it. That's where I was when Maeve called me and asked me to check on you. I had to step out of the meeting to take the call."

All my idea balloons deflated. If Mr. Winger hadn't shot Bob, there didn't seem to be much of a chance that he'd shot Avery. The two events happened too close together to be coincidence, especially considering the similarity in weapons.

I'd come to the wrong place and accused an innocent man. Worse, I'd upset a man who was trying to do the right thing and get his life back together. "I'm sorry. I won't tell anyone."

Mr. Winger nodded, but his expression stayed closed off and guarded.

Keith motioned back toward the parking lot. "I'll meet you in the car, Ed. I just want to talk to Zoe for a minute while you close up."

Mr. Winger nodded again, almost on autopilot.

Keith told hold of my arm and ushered me out of the building. His grip wasn't painful, but it was definitely tight, as if he didn't want to risk me running back into the building to grill Ed Winger further.

He stopped us twenty feet out into the parking lot. He linked his hands together on top of his head, turned back and glanced at Mr. Winger's office again, then swiveled to face me and let his hands drop to his sides.

He opened his mouth, closed it, and rubbed his hands over his face.

My stomach lurched as if I'd tripped and didn't know how hard the landing would be. Was he going to break up with me over this?

"I'm always under a microscope." Keith's voice was controlled. Too controlled. As if he were afraid that if he let even a smidgen of frustration out, he'd lose his temper entirely. But was that anger for me, or for the critics? "Every choice. Every word. You know this. I'm sure you saw it with your dad."

Few people had a closer view of the scrutiny pastors were under than their families. And that scrutiny wasn't entirely unwarranted. Church leaders should be held to a higher standard, but it'd always seemed to me that people looked for reasons to attack and criticize them more often than not. The grace that they wanted extended to themselves, they weren't willing to extend to their pastor and his family.

And that was the people who called themselves Christians. People outside the church were worse. They tried to catch every mistake a pastor or his family made so they could hold it up as proof that Christianity was false. It'd driven me nuts that they couldn't see the logical fallacy in that. The character of the messenger doesn't negate the truth of the message. If a thief was the one to tell me my house was on fire, I shouldn't assume he was lying just because he's a thief.

I yanked my mind back to the present. Where was Keith going with this? "I've seen it. I've lived it. Being a pastor's kid was like living in a petri dish."

"That's what I thought. I thought you'd understand because you'd lived it." A touch of frustration crept into his voice. "As long as we're together, everything you do reflects back on me and on the church, just like it did when your dad was the pastor. Your actions have consequences. If Ed hadn't believed me that I didn't tell you about his addiction, that would have damaged all the work I'd done building that relationship. If word got out, it could have meant others wouldn't trust me, either."

The note of frustration had vanished by the time he'd finished, replaced by a cold logic.

A weird spinning sensation filled my chest, as if I couldn't get my balance. "I couldn't have known you were helping him. It's not fair to blame me for what might have happened when I didn't have enough information to be able to reasonably conclude it was even a risk."

Keith shortened the distance between us and took my hand. "All I'm saying is that, if we're going to have a future, as long as I'm in ministry, we both have to be cautious about what we do."

I stared down at our linked fingers. What if I didn't want to live under such a high level of scrutiny again? Every time I'd left the house as a teenager, there'd been this ball of anxiety in my stomach that I was going to make a mistake and someone was going to see it and judge me—and, by extension, my dad—for it. What I wore. What I said. What I didn't say. Where I went. When I'd moved to the city where no one knew I was a preacher's kid, it'd been like I'd sprouted wings. What if I couldn't go back? Keith and I would be over. He wouldn't give up his calling for me, and I wouldn't want him to.

But what if he was my only chance to get married and have kids? To have someone who'd always be there for me and to be able to choose to be a mom like Camille rather than one like Tonya? And it wasn't like I was a catch. I was well aware that I came with enough baggage to fill a U-Haul. There were no guarantees that if I screwed this up I'd ever find someone else.

My lungs seemed to shrink to half their normal size. Would Keith even still want to be with me if he found out I'd been fired from my previous job for stealing?

All the wires in my brains were sparking. Too much to think about. I couldn't process it all now.

I squeezed his hand. "I'll try."

It was the best I could promise him.

My eyes popped open. The room around me was dark, only vague outlines marking my dresser and the curtains blocking out the streetlights. I hadn't pulled them evenly shut, and a line of light cut down my floor. Star shifted and stretched beside me with a tiny kitty yawn.

What had woken me this time? My phone lay silent on the bedside table, so a middle-of-the-night call wasn't the culprit.

A creak came from downstairs. The old dining room floorboards. Judith must not have been able to sleep. Maybe I should check on her.

I wriggled out of the bed, trying not to disturb Star. Why had I waited so long to have a cat again? Not that Star was officially mine. But she or another cat could be. I would never have to sleep without a cat again if I didn't want to now that Orion and I weren't confined to an apartment.

I tiptoed out of my bedroom. If Orion heard me, he'd want out of his crate at—I glanced at my phone—3:30 in the morning, and he wouldn't easily go back to sleep.

A shadowy figure passed the end of the stairs—the form much too tall to be Judith.

Blood pounded into my head, and I pressed a hand over my mouth to stifle a gasp. Someone was in our house.

One time, when Judith and I were teenagers staying alone overnight for the first time, we'd thought we'd heard someone breaking in. I'd charged out to confront the person while Judith wanted to hide.

This time, hiding seemed like the smartest plan. This intruder could be the same person who'd shot Bob and Avery. I didn't have any weapon that could defend against a gun.

I edged backward, reaching behind me for Judith's doorknob. Slowly, I eased the door open. I couldn't let whoever was down there know I'd spotted him. As soon as I woke Judith, we'd call 911 and hide.

The curtains in her room weren't closed. Light from the streetlamps streamed in. Judith's bed was empty.

My breath stuck in my throat and wouldn't move. Had the intruder already forced Judith from her bed and had her tied up somewhere downstairs? No, I definitely would have heard that.

I needed the police. I dialed 911 and explained to the operator who answered that there was someone in my house.

"Officers are on their way. I'm going to stay on the line with you until they get there."

Maybe Judith was already hiding in her closet. Maybe she'd heard the intruder before I did. But then wouldn't she have already called the police? And even if Judith was terrified, she would have tried to warn me.

I peeked in her closet. Empty.

Oh no. What if she was in the bathroom? I glanced over at her bed. The bed was still made, as if she hadn't come home from the hospital last night. Had she fallen asleep at the hospital?

I edged back into Judith's closet. No sense in making it easier for the intruder to find me if he came upstairs before the police arrived.

Without disconnecting from the 911 operator, I switched over to my text messages. One unread message.

Too tired to drive home. Nurses said I could sleep in the empty bed in Bob's room tonight. Love you.

She'd finished it with a little heart.

I slumped against the wall. Judith was safe.

In the distance, sirens blared to life, heading closer.

"The sirens are going to scare him away." My whispered words came out with a bit of a hiss.

"I'm sorry, ma'am. There must have been a miscommunication somewhere. But they're almost there now. You'll be safe soon."

Safe was fine and good. Yes, get whoever it was out of my house. But the police needed to catch him, too, especially if this was the same person who shot Bob and killed Avery.

"Police," a man's voice shouted out from down below.

"They're here now," I said.

The 911 operator disconnected the call. I came out of the closet, flipped on the lights, and opened the door so the police wouldn't think I was the intruder and shoot me by accident. I crawled up on Judith's bed and sat cross-legged.

Heavy footsteps traveled up the stairs. Detective MacIntosh, wearing a bulletproof vest over his suit, came into the room. He started, then waved the officer with him on down the hall.

"Are you okay?" His gaze ran over me. One corner of his lips twitched.

I glanced down. This week's pajamas were Scooby-Doo, with the words *Ruh-Roh* right across my chest. Yes, buddy, I like silly pajamas. Deal with it. "I'm fine. He didn't see me." I nodded at his ballistic vest. "Have you been demoted?"

He gave me a scowl, but it seemed like it lacked conviction. "I was already at work for another case. When I heard your address, I came along."

A flutter filled my chest. Had he been worried about me, or had he come along because an intruder sounded like it could be the shooter trying to strike again? Not that it mattered.

He took another step into the room. "Where's Judith? The dispatcher said you were the only one in the house."

Right. Judith was his friend. It was Judith he'd been worried about. I was just the annoying woman he worked with occasionally through the shelter, who liked to meddle in his cases. "She stayed at the hospital with Bob tonight."

My words came out flat.

Detective MacIntosh came the rest of the way into the room and knelt down in front of me, putting us at eye level. "You're sure you're alright? Not feeling shaky or cold or detached?"

"I have no symptoms of shock. You don't need to haul me off to the hospital again."

Great. And now I sounded petulant. Why couldn't he go away and search the rest of the house with the other police?

A female officer stepped into the doorway. "Detective?"

Detective MacIntosh rose to his feet and turned to face her. "Yes?"

"Officer Cohen's back. The suspect got away."

I pursed my lips. Of course he got away. They'd warned him they were coming. The intruder was probably out of the door before they even turned onto my street. He wouldn't have even had to run.

Detective MacIntosh thanked her and came back to where I was. He motioned at the bed. "May I sit?"

He did still need to take my witness statement, for what little I saw. Orion was barking softly downstairs. My chances of getting back to sleep seemed nil. I scooted over to make room.

He sat. "I'm going to post officers outside your house for the time being. I think whoever this is might be targeting either you or Judith, and Bob and Avery were accidental casualties."

"That's preposterous." I blurted the words out before I could consider whether saying the word *preposterous* would make me sound exactly that. "I haven't done anything worthy of being shot. I'm not *that* unlikeable."

"I didn't say you're unlikeable." Detective MacIntosh lifted a hand like he wanted to tug at his hair, then caught himself and lowered it back down to his thigh. "Frustrating, absolutely. But not unlikeable. Can you at least listen to me for a second?"

I started to say that his second was already up, but that would have been childish. Instead, I clamped my lips together and glared at him.

He sighed. "Assuming this intruder is the same guy, he's now gone to the shelter—a place you and Judith both frequently go. Then he breaks into the house next door, which he might have mistaken for yours. When he realized his mistake, he came back. Can you think of any other reason someone might have broken in here tonight?"

"Random." I shrugged and tried to keep my face expressionless. I wasn't about to admit that I'd been investigating a little, and that might be why someone had broken in tonight. Besides, both the men I questioned had alibis. I wasn't a big enough threat to either of them for them to take the chance of trying to kill me. "I'm not at the shelter enough for someone to assume I'd be the first one there in the morning. I'm almost never there in the morning, in fact. One of the real shelter employees always opens. And if the shooter wanted Judith, he's doing a bad job. All he would have to do would be to watch her to know she didn't come home tonight."

"We can't assume the shooter was tailing her. He might have believed she came home. That would be her normal routine."

I rubbed a finger against my bottom lip. I had to concede that point. "Judith is the least likely person to have a murderer after her."

Detective MacIntosh raised his eyebrows.

I crossed my arms over my chest. "Other than last time."

My shoulders slumped. Crap. Could he be right? But Judith and Bob both said there weren't any incidents at the shelter lately that would have angered someone enough to kill. Certainly not to kill multiple people.

Star strode into the room and gave a tiny *merr*. She rubbed against Detective MacIntosh's legs. Traitor cat.

He leaned over and stroked her cheek. At least he knew better than to pet an unfamiliar cat all the way down their body. "Is this Ms. Dunhill's cat?"

The air whooshed out of my lungs. Detective MacIntosh had assumed Judith or I must be the real target because we had a link, however tenuous, to all three locations. One other being had a stronger connection. "Star was in all three places."

His eyebrows drew down as if I might indeed be in shock and talking nonsense. "Star?"

I pointed down, and his gaze followed.

He looked back up at me with an are-you-kidding-me expression. "The cat?"

I scooped her up, but she squirmed out of my hold and alternated between head butting me and rubbing against Detective MacIntosh's arm. "She was at the shelter when Bob was shot. Then I fostered her out to Avery, who someone killed. I bring her home with me, and someone breaks into my house. All close together. I think someone wants Star."

"Is there something special about her?"

She was a silver-gray tabby with large, round hazel eyes and a petite build. Definitely adorable, but she also seemed like a regular domestic shorthair. "Not that I know of. I could do a DNA test to see if she's a pure-bred, but she's not secretly carrying a million dollars in uncut diamonds in her stomach if that's what you're asking."

He gave me that look again that said *I can't decide if you're hilarious or weird*. "Then why would someone want her badly enough to kill for her?"

I shrugged. "I don't know. I only realized the connection about thirty seconds ago. But Avery's foster-home paperwork also went missing. We thought it'd been misplaced, but the killer might have taken it to find out who had Star."

Star walked across Detective MacIntosh's lap and stretched up to sharpen her claws on his ballistic vest. His smile burst to life, and my breathing hitched. He really should smile more.

He plucked Star off his lap. "My boss won't like it if

you destroy department property with those tiny sabers of yours."

Star lay down on the bed and licked her paw.

He watched her. "Sadly, your crazy theory is the best we have right now, unless we have a random killer on the loose. If you're right, it's not safe for her to stay here. She's putting you and Judith at risk."

I ran my fingers along Star's soft fur. Removing her from the house felt like abandoning her. Hadn't I lectured Avery on how difficult it is for cats to be shuffled around?

But I had to think about Judith. If it were only me, I'd take the risk. But I couldn't risk Judith's safety. "She can't go back to the shelter, either. She'll be an easy target there. She'll be a target wherever we send her."

A male officer stuck his head in the room. "House and yard are all clear, sir, and the techs are done printing the door and anything that obviously looked like it'd been disturbed."

I shuddered. Was I going to have a huge mess to clean up, or had I heard him before he tossed my house? My parents were going to feel like they should come home for sure after they found out about this. It'd take Judith and I both to talk them out of buying plane tickets when we told them about Avery, followed by the break-in. Maybe they didn't need to know.

My shudder turned into a shiver. Thankfully they hadn't been home. One of them might be dead now.

The officer left.

Detective MacIntosh stood. He didn't seem to notice —or care—that his suit pants were covered in cat fur. "I'll take her home with me, and she can stay in my office at the station when I'm at work until we figure out if she's actually what the intruder was after."

He'd take her? Over my hopefully-not-dead-anytime-soon body. "I can't package her up like a slab of meat and hand her over to you. I'm responsible for her. I need to make sure she'll have a proper environment."

His eyebrows crept up, and his lips twitched in that way that always left me feeling like he was laughing inside. "Are you saying you want to come to my house?"

My cheeks warmed like I was sitting under a heat lamp. Could he get any more exasperating? I didn't want to spend any more time with him than was necessary. "I'm saying she's my responsibility. I can't send her just anywhere."

"I'm not some homeless guy off the street." That mirage of a smile still played around his lips. "You don't trust me?"

The back of my neck tingled. Was he teasing me? If he was anyone else, I'd be sure that's exactly what he was doing. I stood and planted my hands on my hips, even though it meant Scooby-Doo was on full display. "You have a dog. You can't throw a dog and a cat together and hope it works out."

There was something in his eyes I couldn't quite identify. "Then I'll text you my address. I should be home around seven."

16

D etective MacIntosh's house wasn't what I expected. Not a tidy minimalist apartment overlooking the water. Not a townhouse in the new subdivision where every home looked the same except for the cars out front —and sometimes even those matched.

My GPS brought me to a stop at the edge of town in front of a white farmhouse with bright blue shutters and a wraparound porch. The trellis over the front gate burst with red climbing roses, and the air was full of their perfume mingled with the scent of freshly cut grass. The property butted up against fields on two sides, the corn yellow and almost ready for harvest.

How was this the home of pressed-suit, perfectly-styled-hair man? This was the kind of house where you could curl up, reading, on the porch swing in the evenings or spend a rainy afternoon playing board games. It was a home made for laughter. If I could have picked a house for myself, this would have been it.

Maybe he'd rent it to me once he got tired of Arbor and went back to whatever city he'd come from.

Detective MacIntosh came out the front door as if he'd been watching for me. He'd changed out of his suit and into shorts and a t-shirt that revealed his muscular arms. He must have also showered, because the gel was gone from his still-damp hair.

He didn't look like the same man. This guy fit with the house. I could picture him painting the front porch or mowing the grass himself.

My breath did a little hitch. I pulled my gaze away from Detective MacIntosh. No good could come from imagining him doing any of those things. This was a purely professional arrangement.

A three-legged Golden Retriever bounced along beside him, tongue hanging out in that classic smiling expression the breed was known for.

I set down Star's carrier and scratched the dog behind his soft ears. "You have a tripod."

Detective MacIntosh smiled down at the dog, and his expression softened into something almost sad. "This is Cooper." As quickly as the sadness had settled on his face, it was gone. His smile turned mocking. "And he likes cats."

I snorted. The man did not let things go. Star was probably going to fit right in, and he'd make sure to remind me of it for the next five years. "Could you grab her food and the rest of her stuff from my trunk?"

"I already have everything she'll need." He picked up Star's carrier and headed back to the door.

I scrambled after him. I was supposed to be the one in charge here. "The shelter normally supplies the food for animals in foster care."

Detective MacIntosh pushed the door open and waited for me to enter first. "If Cooper and Bella like her, I might keep her. Then she won't be in foster care."

I stepped inside automatically, my legs acting on their own. I'd once wondered why he was always the one helping out the shelter whenever they needed a police officer. None of the tasks were ones requiring a detective. My suspicion had been he was interested in Judith. But maybe he did genuinely love animals and that's why he was so willing.

"Go to your bed, Coop." Detective MacIntosh pointed to a round, fluffy dog bed set off to the side of a brick fireplace. Cooper trundled there and flopped down. "Stay."

He closed the door behind me, set Star's carrier on the floor, and opened her carrier door.

I lunged and scooped her up as soon as she stepped out. "I told you that you can't just let animals free together and hope they work it out. This is why I wouldn't send her home with you without coming myself."

He scowled at me, all the softness that'd been there before gone. "Can you trust me for once? Cooper won't move from that spot until I release him. Not even if a squirrel ran right over his nose."

I pursed my lips. Star squirmed in my arms, trying to break free. "You can't know that."

"I can. He was a police dog until he lost his leg." He

held out his arms toward Star. "Trust me this once. If I'm wrong, you don't ever have to trust me again."

The way he was looking at me and the tone of his voice felt like there were two layers to what he was asking, but I couldn't figure the second one out. What choice did I have, though? Star needed a safe foster home. I slowly handed her over.

He placed her on the ground.

Star strutted straight over to Cooper and sniffed him. Cooper stayed perfectly still, his head resting between his front paws, his eyes focused on Detective MacIntosh as if he wouldn't risk the temptation of so much as looking at Star.

I couldn't even be happy the way I normally would. I could almost feel the gloating waves coming off Detective MacIntosh. "Are you going to say I told you so?"

"Do I need to?" He moved to a closed door off the living room. "Bella is my cat. Alright with you if I let her out?"

Normally I would have said *absolutely not*. There was an order to proper cat introductions. They could take weeks. But Detective MacIntosh did seem to know his pets, and Star had enjoyed the company of other cats at the shelter. "Bella likes other cats?"

"Loves them."

I nodded.

He opened the door. A black cat moved slowly out, her head bobbing and swaying side to side in an awkward way.

"She's blind?"

"Mostly, anyway. When I went to the shelter to pick out a cat a few years ago, she'd just been surrendered with her sister. She followed her sister everywhere, and they figured something was wrong with her. When the vet found her congenital eye condition, they were going to euthanize her. So I took her and her sister. We lost Daisy to cancer before we moved to Arbor. It's been hard for Bella without another cat around."

My chest tightened, as if my heart were suddenly too big to fit. I'd been too harsh on Detective MacIntosh, and I'd made far too many assumptions about him. Clearly I didn't actually know him at all.

Too bad there wasn't any chance of him changing his opinion of me. We might have been able to be friends.

Star crept up to Bella and sniffed her behind. Bella turned around, touched Star's nose by accident, jerked back, then reached out again. Star walked away, with Bella trailing behind her.

My throat tightened, and tears pressed at the back of my eyes. I couldn't take Star back after seeing that. This was her home now. Maybe if I asked nicely, Detective MacIntosh would let me come visit.

I blinked hard. I needed to think about something else, or I was going to start crying in front of him. "How did Cooper lose his leg?"

"A bomb." Detective MacIntosh's voice tightened. "He was a bomb detection dog."

If I looked at Cooper's stump closely, that meant I'd likely find scars beyond what the surgery left. Poor boy.

Brave boy. "You worked the bomb squad before becoming a detective?"

He didn't answer. I glanced over. His gaze wasn't on me. It was on Cooper.

A muscle twitched in his jaw, and his Adam's apple moved up and down as if he were holding back emotion the way I had been earlier. "My brother was. Cooper was his partner."

Was. My arms ached, wanting to hug him and tell him how sorry I was for his loss. Hugging him wouldn't be appropriate, though. And it'd probably be unwanted.

His gaze turned back in my direction and stuck there. His brown eyes felt like they were taking in every angle of my face. My throat went dry. Every angle of my face and probably my makeup-free skin and wild hair and all my other imperfections.

He glanced to the side and cleared his throat. "I owe you an apology."

I swallowed wrong and choked. "Do what now?"

He turned back to me and shook his head. "An apology. You know, one of those things where someone has done something they shouldn't, and they're pretty sure it hurt another person. So they want to ask forgiveness."

My tongue had melded itself to the floor of my mouth. He owed me an apology? For what? He hadn't been wrong when he suggested I could be frustrating and stubborn. He also hadn't been wrong that he could provide a good foster home for Star. If anyone owed anyone else an apology, it was probably me who should be apologizing to him.

But his expression was so serious. He meant it. I worked my tongue loose. "And what would this someone have done that he needs to apologize for?"

"Zoe, come on." The way he said my name—like I'd slapped him.

My breathing tripped again. Did he think I was toying with him to make this harder on him? A spark of anger ignited inside my chest. "You really don't think I'm a good person, do you?"

His eyebrows drew together. "What? I'm trying to say… you really have no idea what I'm talking about?"

Why had I even come here? I didn't need to see his home in person to make sure it was safe for Star. A paper application and an interview like all other foster homes completed would have sufficed.

He was still watching me, expecting me to answer him. I shook my head.

He blew out a breath and ran his hands over his face and up through his hair. Like when he'd taken off his suit, he'd also taken off the forced self-control. "Cooper lost his leg when a bomb unexpectedly exploded. He and my brother were only brought in as a *covering our backs* type of thing. No one expected there to be a bomb in the house."

I shook my head again. I must be exceptionally stupid or desperately sleep deprived. This story didn't seem like it applied to me at all. Or to why he owed me an apology.

"Let me finish." Detective MacIntosh must have read my confusion in my expression. "Okay?"

I nodded. But this would have been easier and less awkward if I could have been petting Cooper while he talked, rather than standing here, feeling exposed in the middle of the room.

"The house belonged to a man who they suspected of two industrial bombings. They finally had enough evidence to arrest him. I interrogated his son, who lived with him. The son insisted he knew nothing about what his father was doing. He seemed clean. Then another factory was bombed while his father was in custody. Everyone, including me, was so sure we'd arrested the wrong man, and that the son was innocent, too, that Cooper and my brother were only sent to the house to quickly cross him off the suspect list."

My head seemed tight and full. I got it now, but he'd asked me to listen to the end.

He moved over to Cooper, stooped down, and petted his head, as if he needed the comfort only an animal could give. "Cooper lost his leg. My brother lost his life. I came to Arbor because I needed to get away from the city. And everything was going exactly how I wanted, until Sebastian Clunes turned up dead, and there you were, with a biological mother in prison for murder, insisting you were innocent."

The painful pieces that had shattered off my heart when he made those accusations months ago knitted themselves back together. What he'd done had made me question whether I could ever be accepted anywhere, let alone in Arbor. I'd never considered he'd acted that way because he was hurting. Not that hurting someone else because you were hurting was right. But it hadn't really been about me, and that made all the difference. He'd been scared to make the same mistake again.

Except... he hadn't entirely misjudged me. He'd been beating himself up over how he'd treated me, but he wasn't wrong. I *was* like Tonya, in some ways.

"I was fired from my last job for stealing." The words were out before I could stop them or second-guess them.

My stomach tumbled like I'd tripped down a flight of stairs. Admitting that to him could be a major mistake. My parents didn't know. Keith didn't know.

And whatever reconciliation he and I had been edging toward would be gone now.

I covered my face. I couldn't stand to see his expression change from repentant to justified. "You're apologizing because you think you wronged someone innocent. I didn't kill Sebastian, but I did cheat and steal. So you don't need to feel bad. I am, technically, a criminal, even if I didn't go to jail for it. I'm not that far from what you thought I was."

I stopped and sucked in a breath. My chest seemed a little lighter, as if I'd been storing all that up and now I didn't have to carry it around. Now he knew the kind of person I was, that I wasn't really as different from Tonya as I wanted to pretend to be.

I dropped my hands from my face, grabbed the cat carrier, and beelined for the door. "Thanks for taking Star and keeping her safe."

"Wait."

Really, he couldn't just let me go? I didn't need a lecture. I didn't need to see that those little hints of possible friendship I'd thought I was seeing were gone. All I needed was to be somewhere else.

"Why?" I spun around. The cat carrier bumped into my leg and sent a dart of pain down the side. "You were right about me in the beginning. You don't need to apologize or feel bad. What else is there to say?"

"That you accept my apology."

I focused on his face. His expression had gone still again. To maintain professional distance now that he knew what I was, or to keep from spooking me? Because my urge to run was strong right now. My heart beat so fast in my chest that all the beats sort of melded together.

I sucked in a deep breath, pulling in the air until my lungs ached, then let it go. I didn't have to be reactive. I could control myself. I could use my words. Or so my therapist liked to tell me. "I don't understand."

He moved closer so that five feet rather than the length of the room separated us. "I acted unprofessionally because of my own emotions. That was wrong regardless of who you were. I made assumptions without enough evidence, and that's bad police work. And I already knew about the theft. So you telling me about it now doesn't change anything."

I opened and closed my mouth, but nothing came out. Of course he'd known about the theft. He'd run me through the system when he brought me in for questioning about Sebastian's murder. My employer dropped everything and settled for firing me because the rest of the staff advocated for me. But it would still be in my record.

He'd already known. "Did my record say why I did it?"

Star hopped up on the couch. Bella followed her. They didn't curl up together, but they both laid down on their own cushions. It wouldn't take them long to move to the next step. Sometimes two personalities just clicked with each other.

Detective MacIntosh followed my gaze. "The records said you claimed you'd done it because too many people weren't able to afford the medications for their pets. You and another employee started cutting the costs despite what the corporate owner wanted you to charge. I wouldn't have personally called it theft. It was more like fraud."

A laugh built up in my chest. "I don't think that's much better."

"Not from a legal perspective." He shrugged. "But you were punished for your crime by losing your job, so it's not like you got away with anything."

True. And it wasn't something I'd do again. Faced with the same situation, I'd find another solution. Hopefully now that I was a partner in my own veterinary clinic, I'd never have to.

He smiled at me. "So?"

My heart bumped into the front of my chest. This time I knew what he wanted, but there was no harm in teasing him a little. "So?"

He glowered at me, but he couldn't quite get rid of his smile. "I'm still waiting to hear if I'm forgiven for our first couple of meetings."

The catharsis of the last few minutes made it feel more like I should be thanking him for the therapy session than forgiving him, but hearing the words seemed important to him. "I forgive you, Detective."

"Haven't we known each other long enough to be on a first-name basis instead of titles?"

My cheeks warmed. Calling him Ryan seemed strangely intimate. Which was ridiculous. Most of the people I knew, I called by their first names. "Maybe."

He rolled his eyes. "Do you have time for pancakes before work? I can make either blueberry or chocolate chip."

My stomach rumbled. "Would it be rude to ask for both?"

He took the cat carrier from me and set it back on the ground. "I think you just did."

17

"**H**e's here!"

Judith's squeal cut through Bob's house from where she'd stationed herself beside the front door. I jumped and nearly lost hold of the spoon I'd been using to stir the tortellini and spinach soup. Judith and I had made dinner at home and then brought everything here to warm up to celebrate Bob's release from the hospital.

I turned the soup down low and joined Judith at the front door.

She peered out the window. "I still think we should have gotten balloons."

"Too dangerous for the cats."

Outside, Keith opened the car door for Bob. After his time in the hospital, Bob looked no worse than someone with a broken arm would have—which had to be our prayers answered. Originally, the doctors warned Judith about all sorts of possible complications, including infection.

We threw open the door and held up the *Welcome Home* banner Judith made. The grin on Bob's face was worth every second she put into it. The smile she gave him in return was radiant.

I glanced between them. Age gap or no, there was definitely something going on here, at least on Judith's side. I hadn't asked her about it because I didn't want to put ideas in her head if they weren't already there, but maybe it was time.

We ushered the men inside, and the four of us sat around the table and ate soup, fresh bread, and peach pie until we were stuffed.

Bob finished his last bite of pie. "Have you decided what to do next about Harper?"

I'd filled him in about my call with Children's Aid the last time I'd visited.

My bite of pie stuck in my throat, and I took a sip of water. "I don't have many paths. Either I have to go speak to Tonya and hope she'll give me Harper's full name and date of birth or I have to give up."

Keith got up and collected everyone's plates. "You used to go every year. This isn't much different."

Judith shot me a look that said *Don't bite his head off.* "It was horrible every year. Tonya was either passive-aggressive, telling Zoe how awful her life in prison was and then saying how she hoped Zoe was having fun. Or she criticized everything about Zoe—her clothes, her weight, her skin."

I scurried to the coffee maker to give myself something to do. Tears pushed at the backs of my eyes. If I'd said all that, I could have been brushed off as overreacting. But when someone else pointed out how Tonya used to treat me, it made it harder for people who hadn't been there to deny the reality of her behavior.

"I hope you don't mind me giving my two cents," Bob said. "But I think you should still try to get Harper's information from her." He nodded toward my hands. "Do you need help with that?"

I glanced down. I'd scooped the coffee out, but I hadn't put it into the coffeemaker. I finished and started the coffee brewing. "I'm fine."

I sat back down in my chair.

Keith came behind me and squeezed my shoulders. "I didn't realize what she was like. You don't talk about her much."

When you'd come out of an abusive situation, one of the worst parts was having people not believe it'd been as bad as it was. He couldn't know how much that acknowledgment meant, especially after how tense things had been between us after the confrontation outside Mr. Winger's office.

I put my hands over his. He stayed standing behind me.

Bob adjusted his sling. He grimaced slightly. "I know what it was like for me wondering if I had siblings or not. A couple months ago, Judith finally convinced me to take one of those DNA tests, and I'm glad I listened to her. Turns out I have two half siblings, but that my dad had recently passed away."

Judith touched his arm. He smiled softly at her. It

wasn't the kind of smile that said the story had a happy ending.

"If I'd hunted for him earlier, I might have gotten the chance to say all the things I wanted to say to him. I know you'd only be going to get information about Harper, but it might give you a chance at some closure with Tonya, too."

I harrumphed. "You don't know Tonya. Letting myself hope she's changed will only lead to worse heartache. I spent all my teenage years hoping she'd change. She didn't, and there isn't anything left for me to say to her. I said it all in a letter I wrote her on my eighteenth birthday, explaining why I wouldn't be visiting her again. My therapist said I'd feel better if I did that rather than simply terminating our visits as soon as I wasn't obligated by the courts to go anymore."

"I remember that letter." Judith cringed. "You had me read it to make sure you were clear. Running her over with a truck couldn't have been clearer."

"Probably not my finest hour, but I had a lot of teenage rage."

Judith mouthed the words *Zoe the Volcano* at me, but she didn't say them out loud.

I chuckled, but the bubble of mirth quickly popped. "It didn't work anyway, if you remember. She wrote me a long letter back minimizing and explaining away and shifting blame."

Keith came around and slid into the chair next to me. He picked my hand back up as if he wanted me to know that nothing from my story so far had scared him away. The urge to snuggle into him and kiss him washed over me. But kissing him in front of others would have made him uncomfortable. PDAs were absolutely not his thing. I settled for tightening my grip on his hand.

"What about your siblings?" I asked Bob.

"Never responded when I contacted them. But I can't blame them. We're all midway through our lives and established. Harper's still young. You still have a chance that she'll want to be a part of your life. If you let Tonya take that away from you, I think you'll regret it."

The rich aroma of coffee filled the air along with the peaceful dripping sound as the coffee percolated. I drew in a lungful of the scent. If someone could bottle the smell of freshly brewed coffee, they could sell it as a balm for frayed nerves.

Keith must have caught my longing glance at the coffee pot because he got up and filled mugs.

I clasped my hands together in my lap. Tonya had stolen a lot from me, not the least of which was a normal childhood. Then I'd made my own series of bad decisions afterward. So many things about my past I couldn't change and wished I could. If I didn't visit Tonya and at least try, Harper could end up on that list.

Harper probably didn't even know about me yet, but what if she found out in the future? What if she realized I'd known about her, had the opportunity to find her, but hadn't taken it? The rejection of that would leave a sting that time might not be able to heal. In her life story, I'd become the sister who hadn't wanted her, playing a role right alongside the mother who hadn't valued her enough to pull her life together.

This wasn't only about me. Harper mattered, too. She was my sister just like Judith was, and so it was my job to take care of her if I could. I had to do this for her, even more than for myself.

18

Maeve swiveled her computer chair around, turning her back on the order sheet she'd been updating. "A cat. You think two people got shot over a cat. That's far-fetched even for you."

Some days the desire to stick my tongue out at Maeve was almost overwhelming. The only thing that made up for it was the rest of the time when you couldn't have asked for a better friend or business partner.

"Not necessarily." Tyler tossed the IV bag he'd swapped out into the trash and opened the cupboard where we kept the medications. "My mom breeds Serengeti cats. When a new breed gets TICA, CFA, or FIF accreditation, and you're one of the few breeders at the forefront, you can easily get $2,000 to $3,000 per kitten. The price comes down as more breeders enter the game."

My mouth drooped open, and I snapped it shut. I knew purebred dogs often cost that much, but I hadn't realized kittens could as well. With an average litter size of three to five kittens, a queen of a new breed could be a lucrative investment, especially since cats were less expensive to care for than dogs.

Maeve rolled her eyes. "And this cat, who's so valuable, somehow ended up in our shelter."

I inserted the tube of blood for the sample I needed to test into the automated blood analyzer. "Stranger things have happened."

Tyler shrugged and poured a pill out into his hand. "I have a friend who works at one of those pet DNA companies that tell you what your cat or dog has in them. He'd put a rush on her swab if you wanted."

Detective MacIntosh—Ryan—had thought the theory was reasonable enough that he'd taken Star to live with him. And I was her veterinarian. If anyone was going to figure out why someone might be willing to kill for her, it should be me. "Why not? Let me text Ryan and see if I can pick her up for some tests."

Calling him *Ryan* out loud felt as weird as I'd imagined it would. But it was nice, too. Like we might actually be able to be friends now that we'd cleared the air. That would certainly make things less awkward going forward.

Maeve glanced my way, and her eyes narrowed. She never missed anything, which meant that she'd make some comment about me switching to his first name later, when we were alone.

Tyler grinned and headed to the back with the medication.

Can I have a key to your house? I texted Ryan.

Maeve closed what she was working on and came over. "Make sure he knows I'm not the one wasting his time."

I pulled the slide I'd been looking at from the microscope and took it to the sink. "You didn't think it was wasting his time when we were bringing him information that might help solve Sebastian's murder."

"That was different. Those were legitimate leads." She glanced at my phone and did a double-take. She pointed a finger at it. "Maybe you want to rethink that text. 'Can I have a key to your house?' There are a lot of ways a person could take that, and *I want to pick up your foster cat to run some tests* probably isn't high on most people's lists."

My mouth went dry. Crap. She was right. I lunged for my phone.

Response dots that said he was writing an answer were already flashing on the screen.

I want to pick up Star for some tests. I typed so quickly that what I actually ended up sending was *I want pick up stare for some tests.*

I pressed the heel of my hand to my forehead. That was only marginally better. But at least I didn't sound like I was trying to move in with him or something.

My phone pinged, indicating he'd replied.

I backed away slightly.

"Oh for heaven's sake." Maeve scooped my phone up. "You'd think you were some teenager with a crush rather than a mature woman who's already in a committed relationship." She glanced at the screen. "He says it's his day off so he'll bring her here. He also asked if you'd been drinking."

He was absolutely going to regret extending the proverbial olive branch at this point. "Are you serious?"

"No." Maeve slid my phone back across the counter to me. "But you seemed like you needed some sense shocked into you. What kind of tests are we going to run? If we're doing this, we might as well do it right."

She picked up the remaining medicine bottles Tyler had removed from the cupboard and headed for the back, presumably to help him finish more quickly.

I grabbed my phone. She'd been telling the truth. Ryan's message only said that he'd bring Star to the clinic.

"X-rays at least," I yelled after Maeve, even though she hadn't probably meant for me to answer her question. "In case she has diamonds implanted under her skin. And blood work. Maybe someone's designing a biological weapon, and she's the incubator."

"Are any of those things actually possible?" Ryan's voice asked from the direction of the waiting room.

I yelped, fumbled my phone, and barely caught it before it flew from my hands. I set it safely back on the counter. We really needed to install a bell over the door.

I headed for the waiting room. "Did you teleport here?"

His lips twitched in that almost-smile of his. "I was already out running errands, and I have to take her with me wherever I go. I don't think she has diamonds under her skin, for the record. She's too soft when I pet her."

I forced my face into a serious expression. "We can't rule out anything at this point."

"Next you'll be telling me the diamonds were actually crushed up and hidden in her litter box."

Maeve pushed open the door between the reception area and the back of the clinic. "Don't encourage her. Are we going to do this or not?"

***

Tyler's friend was so excited about being a part of our investigation that he drove down to swab Star's cheek himself. He had the results back for us before we'd finished all of our own tests. Star was what, in the dog world, would be known as a mutt.

"That's probably for the best." Tyler had edged closer and closer to Maeve over the course of the past hour until he was now leaning on the counter next to where she stood, so close that he could have smelled her hair by leaning down slightly. "The shelter spayed her, so if she was supposed to help spearhead a new breed, the breeder would be disappointed."

"And there'd have been no reason for anyone who wanted her for breeding purposes to try to get her back." Maeve shifted, and her shoulder bumped Tyler's. She shot straight up and moved over a couple inches. "Which I tried to tell everyone from the start."

I grinned and peered closer at the x-rays I was examining to hide it. Tyler had taken me at my word when I told him to stop pestering Maeve, but he was doing everything else possible, like subtly invading her personal space. The man was determined, I'd give him that.

Ryan moved next to me. He smelled like pine and fresh air. What did he do—roll around under the trees in his yard each morning? "No diamonds, I'm guessing."

"No diamonds." I added fake sadness to my voice.

Unfortunately for the case but fortunately for Star, there wasn't anything else unusual on her x-rays, either. They could have been included in a textbook showing what a healthy cat's body looked like. Her blood tests had all been normal as well, which Maeve was intolerably smug over since she'd argued we didn't need to run blood tests.

I switched x-rays to the final view. Textbook again. Almost.

"Tyler, does this look like a microchip to you?"

He came up on the other side of me. "Yup. Right between the shoulder blades where it should be."

I shook my head. "The shelter checks for chips when an animal comes in. She didn't have one. At least not one that showed up on the chip reader."

Ryan got Star back out of her carrier, and Maeve grabbed the scanner. We took turns running it over the spot where the x-rays showed Star's microchip nestled. Nothing.

Ryan returned her to her carrier. "Do chips often malfunction?"

"Only about 0.4 percent of the time." I set the scanner back on the counter. "It's more often a case of using a scanner with the wrong frequency, but ours is universal." I swept a hand in Star's direction. "But, obviously, a 0.4 percent chance isn't a zero percent chance."

Maeve returned the scanner to the proper shelf. "That only means she might have an owner out there somewhere, missing her. It doesn't tell us anything about why someone would want her badly enough to kill for her."

Star had curled up in her carrier, peaceful in a way that most cats weren't when confined, especially after being poked and examined.

"Microchip failure is rare." The idea started to form as I spoke the words. "So whoever was after Star might have assumed that her microchip was still functioning, and they could get information off of it if they snatched her. They might not have even wanted to take her, only to scan her chip, but people kept getting in the way."

"Because that information would lead them to someone they were trying to find," Ryan said, finishing my thought. His tone of voice said he was considering the idea rather than brushing it off.

I nodded.

His gaze was intent on me now. "How do we find out who that person might be with the microchip not working?"

"I can take it out." Poor little Star. As if she hadn't gone through enough lately. "It'll have a serial number on it. Then it'll be up to you to follow the trail."

19

I drove my car slowly along the fence of the women's correctional facility where Tonya lived. It looked exactly the way I remembered it, surrounded by open land on all sides, with only a few trees. The watchtower overlooking the grounds was still the same puke-brown. As a teenager, I'd been surprised that it looked like the ones in movies. Not a lot of things in movies actually matched real life.

I swallowed the last gulp of my now-cold coffee. I should have stopped at the Starbucks a couple hours back, but the idea of putting this task off even a few more minutes was unbearable. The sooner I went in, the sooner this was over. I wasn't a teenager anymore with a self-esteem she could easily shatter. She could play all the belittling games she wanted so long as she gave me Harper's information.

I turned off my car and marched for the gate. I went

through the sign-in procedure and left my phone and other personal belongings locked in a rented locker.

A guard showed me to a seat in front of a plexiglass barrier. Tonya's murder conviction meant her visits were no-contact, which was a blessing. My skin crawled at the mere thought of having to touch her.

The chair was hard, as if they didn't want people to get too comfortable.

My heart beat erratically, and my vision blurred slightly, then cleared. I wasn't supposed to have to do this ever again. It was like Tonya had withheld information about Harper for this very reason. So she'd still have one last way of getting to me.

A buzzer sounded, and the door on the far side of the room opened. Tonya shuffled through, escorted by a guard.

My lungs froze and wouldn't draw in air. How had I forgotten how much I looked like her?

Same athletic build. Same wavy dark hair, though hers was frizzier than mine, almost closer to curly. Same oval face. Same lips, though I prayed to God mine didn't always carry that mocking tilt to them.

At least I'd gotten my dad's green eyes. Otherwise, this would be too close to looking at a picture of my future that would be inevitable. And whatever else happened, I refused to follow Tonya's path.

She sat and picked up the phone on her side. I mirrored her action and picked up the phone on my side, my hand moving like a robot controlled by someone else.

"Do I know you?" Her voice was still silky smooth.

Despite all her other vices, Tonya had never smoked. She'd been too vain for it, not wanting to stain her fingers or her teeth. Not wanting to smell like anything other than cheap perfume.

Hot anger built inside me, bubbling.

She stared straight through the glass at me. No way she didn't recognize me. I stared back.

The wrinkles in her forehead and around her eyes popped out at me. When had she gotten so old? The beauty she'd clung to was still there but in ragged tatters of what it used to be. Unlike Camille, the woman who'd taken the role of mom in my life, Tonya's wrinkles weren't beautiful in their own right, the sign of days spent laughing and nights spent worrying over those she loved. Tonya's were more like the lies and hard living catching up to her and making her look outside like what she'd always been inside.

My anger fizzled slightly. Tonya would never know what she'd missed. And I'd had Camille, my real mom, not just a woman who'd given birth to me. I'd gotten the better end of this deal.

Tonya tapped a finger on the plexiglass. Hard. *Rap. Rap.* "You look familiar, a little like an ungrateful daughter I used to have. But it's been so long since she's been here that I was sure she was dead."

"I'm obviously not dead." I bit the inside of my cheek. *Stop it, Zoe. Trading barbs with her won't get you anywhere.* "How have you been?"

"I've been in prison. No visits to break the monotony. No one putting money on my commissary account so I can buy the little things that would make life more bearable."

You killed someone, I wanted to shout. *This is punishment, not a vacation.*

My dad liked to say that God put us in situations he knew would grow our character. This had to be one of those moments. What other purpose could there be for making me go through this?

I forced my lips into a smile that I could only hope didn't look as natural as if I were clamping my teeth around a pencil. "I can add something to your account before I leave. Do they have those Swedish fish you used to love?"

"How's your father? He still judging people and trying to tell them how to live?"

Her favorite topics were clearly still her favorite topics. I'd been three when my dad got an impaired driving charge. Not his first. He'd taken court-mandated rehab in lieu of prison. The program was run by a Christian organization, and my dad gave his life to Jesus. I'd been able to hear Tonya yelling at him through the walls, through the blanket I'd hidden under, when he told her that he wanted them both to quit doing drugs and get married. Apparently, he'd never stop being the villain in Tonya's life story.

I set down the phone and pressed my fingers into a line above my eyebrows, massaging the pressure points there. Rehashing old arguments wasn't why I was here. I couldn't. I'd get drawn down the rabbit hole of defending my dad, defending Camille, defending myself, and then the visitation period would be over and I wouldn't be any closer to finding Harper.

I straightened and picked the phone back up. "I'm not here to talk about Dad. I want to know about my sister."

She opened her eyes in feigned surprise, but her lips curled up in a smile. "What sister? I know you have a step-sister. Janice? Josie?"

Lord, give me patience. "I don't mean Judith. I mean Harper." I gritted my teeth. I had to do this. "Will you please tell me about Harper?"

"Ahh." The smile died on her face. "So you finally decided to care about her, did you?"

"I didn't even know about her." My words came out in a yell.

The nearby guard leveled a warning glare at me. I slumped. This was not going well. How could I fix it? There wasn't a way to fix it. Tonya was who she was. I hadn't known how to deal with her as a kid, and I still didn't.

She leaned forward and poked a finger at the glass. "What will you give me if I tell you what you want to know?"

I tamped down on any response. If she'd decided she was willing to trade information about Harper for something, I couldn't let her see I'd happily do that. As soon as she thought something made me happy, she'd rip it away again. "I already said I'd put money on your commissary account. I'll make sure it's enough to keep you in Swedish fish and lipstick for a month."

She tilted her head to the side, her gaze moving over my face. "And then I'll never hear from you again. No, I don't think so. I want visits again."

A voice inside my head that sounded a lot like the child me screamed and wouldn't stop.

One and done. That's what this was supposed to be. Not locking me in forever, so I could never get free.

My hands shook. The tremors traveled down my arms and through the rest of my body.

I pulled in a breath and held it until my lungs burned. I eased it out. Harper was a minor. So she was probably required to visit Tonya once a year like I'd been. We could go together. That would help her and make it easier for me. "I'll come once a year like before as long as you tell me, truthfully, everything I want to know about Harper, including her last name and birthday."

Her gaze hardened and locked on mine. "Once a month."

She had to be joking. "No. Absolutely not."

She wrapped the cord of the phone around her finger. "That's fine. But don't think you'll find her without me. You've already tried everything you can think of or you wouldn't be here. You never could do anything right."

This had been a mistake.

I slammed the phone into its cradle. I'd find another way to locate Harper. There had to be another way. Anything would be better than making a deal with that she-devil.

20

My phone rang as I was liberating it from the locker. If it was Judith, I'd let it go to voicemail and text her that I was on my way home. Speaking to her would mean crying, and crying and driving were a bad combination.

The screen said *Detective MacIntosh*. *Him* I could talk to. He didn't even know where I was.

I answered the call and headed for my car.

"I found Star's owner," he said as soon as we finished the hellos.

A zing flashed through me, but tears stung my eyes. I should be all smiles. Returning a lost pet to their owner was the dream situation every time a creature was brought into the shelter as a stray.

I blinked rapidly. This was why I didn't normally foster. Stupid attachment instinct. Last time I'd fostered, I ended up naming the dog Orion, and we hadn't been parted for more than a day since. The couple of animals who'd come through our house as fosters since then had been for medical reasons and Judith had been the one responsible for them.

"I didn't need to get a warrant," Ryan was saying. "The company who makes the microchips had a rep call the pet ID company who manages them. They called the owner, and she got back to me with her address this morning."

I climbed into my car and slumped down. The heaviness in my body wouldn't seem to lift. "I'm sorry about Bella losing her friend."

"I'm hoping you'll help me find another cat friend for her. I shouldn't have left her alone so long. She does better with another cat."

Two options immediately popped into my mind. Both were mature cats who'd have a harder time getting adopted but who loved being around the other cats at the shelter. "I can meet you at the shelter later today if you'd like."

That would give me something nice to look forward to at least.

The clicking sound of him signaling a turn came through the phone. He must have me on Bluetooth. "That's why I'm calling, actually. I'm in the car now, heading to return Star, and I thought you might like to come with me. You're the one who found the microchip. You're the one who should be there to reunite her with her family."

Seeing Star back with the people who'd been missing

her and worried about her would ease the loss. There was only one problem. "I'd like to, but I'm not in Arbor."

"I can pick you up. Where are you?"

His tone was so open and friendly—the exact opposite of how it'd been when we met. I'd always thought Judith was seeing him through her perpetual rose-colored glasses when she talked positively about him. But I could see it now.

If I told him my location, would that change everything? Here I was, visiting the person I'd claimed to be nothing like and want nothing to do with.

He was smart. Even if I only told him the city, as a police officer, he'd make the connection.

So I could either lose this opportunity that I wanted and go home to drown this day in whatever ice cream and cookies I could find in our house… or I could take the risk and hope he wouldn't reject me out of hand.

So how much did I want this friendship? There couldn't be one if I didn't tell him where I was now. We'd be acquaintances. We'd be cordial. But you couldn't have a real friendship if you never trusted your friends with the ugly bits.

The memory of how easy it'd been to talk to him while we shared the pancakes he made flashed across my mind.

I did want this friendship. A lot.

There also wouldn't be a friendship if he couldn't handle where I was. But that part was on him. I could only take responsibility for me.

"I'm in Huron Valley at the Women's Correctional Facility."

The crunch of gravel filled his side of the call, then quiet except for a soft clicking. His signal? Had he pulled off the road?

I leaned my head on the steering wheel. He was going to withdraw the offer. Or he was coming up with some snarky comment. And I couldn't stay here and cry when he did. If I sat in my car too long, a guard would come out and ask me to leave the parking lot. Maybe I should get going now, so I could at least find a safe spot to park somewhere else.

"According to the GPS," Ryan's voice sounded slightly distracted, as if he were looking at the GPS at that moment, "Star's owner lives about a half hour past where you are. Do you want to wait there for me or start driving back and meet me somewhere along the way?"

My throat thickened to the point where I wasn't sure I could get the words out. "There's a Starbucks about half-way. I'll wait there and get us both a coffee. I don't know about you, but I could really use one."

"Text me the address."

The silence stretched with only the sound of his clicker filling it while I did as he asked, but he didn't disconnect, and neither did I.

"Are you okay?" His words were soft.

No. Absolutely not okay. But now wasn't the time to get into it.

"I will be." I tried to laugh, but it came out garbled, more like a turkey gobble. "I'll see you in an hour."

***

Star's owner, Melanie, threw open the door before we even had a chance to knock or ring the doorbell. She was in her late thirties or early forties, with sleek honey-blonde hair pulled back in a ponytail.

She waved her hands in big arcs. "Come in."

We followed her inside. Ryan set Star's carrier down.

Melanie dropped to her knees beside the carrier. She looked up at Ryan. "May I take her out?"

He wore his suit with his badge clipped to the belt. No wonder she felt like she had to ask permission.

He smiled. "Of course. She's your cat, ma'am."

Melanie opened the carrier, and Star crawled right into Melanie's arms. Unlike when any of us tried to hold her, she snuggled in under Melanie's chin, her purrs loud enough to hear five feet away.

Melanie dipped her head, burying her face in Star's fur. "I don't know how to thank you. She's been gone almost four months. I was starting to wonder if I should give up and adopt another cat, especially since she went missing right before I moved. She'd never have found her way back to me on her own."

Ryan and I both mumbled something about how it was our pleasure and our job and so on.

Melanie lifted her head slightly. Star stretched up and rubbed her face against Melanie's chin as if making sure she wasn't going too far away.

Melanie grinned, then her gaze flickered to Ryan's badge. "Is it normal for a police detective to return a missing cat?"

I opened my mouth to answer, then snapped it shut. Nope. Ryan let me do my job running all kinds of tests on Star to see if we could figure out why someone might want her. I'd let him do his job rather than running in and stomping on his toes. That only seemed fair.

His face took on the serious, professional expression I was used to seeing. He explained what had happened and how we found Star's malfunctioning microchip. "We weren't able to find any reason why someone would want your cat badly enough to kill for her. I'm here to see if you know a reason."

Melanie's face went slack as he spoke. She moved backwards mechanically. "I'm sorry. I need to sit."

She backed away until she reached her living room couch. She dropped onto it and wrapped her body around Star as if that would protect her.

Ryan followed after her, so I followed him.

Melanie sucked her bottom lip between her teeth until it almost disappeared. She let it go. "I had a stalker. I got a restraining order, but"—she looked up at Ryan from her position on the couch—"well, you know. The laws around stalkers are too weak."

I glanced at Ryan. He was nodding. Anything I knew about stalkers came from movies—not the most reliable source—but, even there, restraining orders often tended to make the stalker more determined. They almost never protected the person they were meant to protect.

"The officer I was assigned to finally suggested that I consider moving. He said I needed to do it in a way that couldn't be traced. Sell my furniture. Take only what I could pack quickly in my car. Don't tell anyone where I was going until enough time had passed for him to give up and fixate on someone else."

My fingers went cold. How awful that the only way to get rid of a threat was to hope that threat decided you were too much work and went to threaten someone else.

Melanie snuggled her face into Star again. "Tinsel went missing the day before I planned to move. I thought about staying. I wanted to stay. But I'd already sold my house, and the new owners were coming in. I stayed with my sister for an extra week even, but then I couldn't risk her family anymore."

Tinsel—so that was Star's real name.

"I couldn't even update my address with the pet ID people." Her words had picked up speed. "I drove to Ohio and bought a cheap SIM card for a new phone and added that number so there wouldn't be an area code to trace to me, just in case. My stalker worked in web design. I wasn't sure how much he'd be able to hack."

She'd turned her life upside down to escape him, only to find that he might still be hunting for her months later. Not only hunting for her. Hunting for her and angry enough to kill anyone who stood in the way of finding her. Who knew what someone like that would do if he finally found her?

I wrapped my hands into fists. How did Ryan deal with this day after day? People like Melanie that he couldn't always protect. People who lost their children that he couldn't find. People like Ellery, whose loved ones had been murdered, and the murderer wasn't caught.

We couldn't let this guy get away with it. For Ellery's sake. For Melanie's sake. This time we had to make sure the evil person behind all of this was caught.

Melanie had squished her eyes shut, but tears slipped out anyway. "Could he have been trying to find me through Tinsel?"

"We're not sure, ma'am." Ryan's voice carried a tone that would have put anyone at ease. "But I'm going to personally contact local law enforcement and ask them to keep an officer on your house until we're sure. In the meantime, I'd like you to tell me everything you can about your stalker."

21

Ryan and I walked back to his car in silence. He opened the car door for me, as if he knew this had been harder on me than on him because I wasn't used to it. And maybe because he remembered how shaky I'd sounded earlier.

He turned on the car and pulled back out onto the road. "So what do you think? I'm sure you have plenty of opinions."

His tone was teasing. Not a putdown, but rather an acknowledgment and acceptance that this was who I was. I was someone who had opinions on things, and that wasn't likely to change. There was comfort in that. And freedom. A month ago, I'd have said that he didn't know how to be nice.

I settled back into the seat. "I have questions. Like how did the stalker know where her cat was if she didn't? That doesn't fit with the stalker theory."

"That crossed my mind, too." He kept his gaze on the

road and navigated back onto the highway. "Stalkers can be creative when it comes to getting what they want. When he realized she was planning to move and he might not be able to follow her, he could have stolen her cat. Her old address with the pet ID company was much closer to Arbor. Assuming the stalker lived near her original address, it would explain why Star was found in Arbor."

Trees and bushes zipped past outside. Who would have thought this would be how my day turned out? No closer to knowing how to find Harper, but Star—Tinsel, more accurately—back with her mom. And maybe one step closer to figuring out who shot Bob and Avery and broke into my house.

"So he stole her cat, hoping she'd update the pet ID site with her new address, and he could find her that way?"

"That's what I'm thinking. She did say her stalker worked in web design. Or he might have planned on grabbing Melanie when she showed up to claim her missing cat. According to the person I spoke to, most of the time, if someone finds a cat, the pet ID company connects the finder and the owner. They meet to exchange the pet. He could have pretended to be someone else, so she wouldn't know it was him until it was too late."

I wrapped my arms around my stomach. No one could relax knowing they were being hunted. Afraid to walk alone. Jumping every time a car door slammed or the phone rang. Every creak in the house at night meaning they'd come for you. The year I'd lived that way, when Tonya was out of jail after her first sentence and my dad was afraid she might try to kidnap me, had been enough. I'd wanted to throw a party the day she was arrested for the second time.

I shook off the past's grasping tentacles. "Star must have gotten loose, and he's been trying to get her back ever since." I shifted in my seat so I was facing him instead of the window. "Since she gave you his name, you're going to get his address from the department that handled the stalking case and go talk to him?"

He glanced in my direction and raised an eyebrow as if to say *Obviously*.

He was still an insufferable man sometimes, even if we were friends now.

Silence fell between us, and I went back to watching the landscape through the window. The morning's visit with Tonya played over and over in my mind again. What could I have done or said differently to make her give me Harper's information? Would anything have worked? Tonya always had an agenda of her own and— "Can we talk about something? Anything?"

My words burst out in a rush. The *what ifs* were going to eat me alive if I didn't stop them.

The rustle of fabric told me Ryan had glanced in my direction. "Sure." His tone was cautious. "You want to tell me what had you so upset when I first called this morning?"

Maybe having a detective as a friend wasn't a great

idea after all. He was trained to read people. That'd get annoying fast. "Something else."

"You said *anything*. And that seems to be what you most need to talk about."

I huffed out a breath of air and turned back to face him. He had both hands on the wheel, in perfect driving posture, and his gaze was still safely on the road, but his expression said he was listening. "Has anyone ever told you that you're annoying when you're right?"

"You've never said it before, but you've made it clear you feel that way." His tone was a little tease and a little nudge.

This friendship had definitely been a terrible idea. "Do you ever wonder why God allows evil?"

His gaze shifted to me for a split second. "We can't have true freedom without the possibility for evil. The police could lock up any kids who show even a hint of criminal tendencies so they could never commit a crime in the future, but we wouldn't live in a free society anymore." We were long past the turnoff to the Woman's Correctional Facility, but he glanced in that direction. "But I don't think you're looking so melancholy over a theological question."

I sighed and told him the whole story about the inheritance that allowed me to become a partner with Maeve in the vet clinic and also revealed that I had a half-sister I never knew about. I shared everything I'd done to find her and how the only solution had finally been to visit Tonya, who I hadn't seen in over a decade. And how she'd refused to give me anything unless I agreed to resume our visits, monthly this time instead of yearly.

When I finally finished, I sucked in a deep breath. How long had I been talking? Talk about overshare. We'd been friends all of a couple of days, and I go and spill out all that. He was going to think I was some kind of needy, clingy—

"Thank you for trusting me enough to tell me that. That couldn't have been easy after how I treated you before."

After how he'd... oh, right. "I wasn't thinking about that at all. You explained, and I forgave you. I've certainly needed enough second chances in my life. I'd be a hypocrite if I held it over you." I gave him a teasing glare-smile. "I don't give third chances, though, so..."

He chuckled. The sound chipped some of the tension out of my muscles.

And then he didn't say anything else.

I squirmed. "So?"

"So?"

"Aren't you going to tell me what you think I should do? I'm sure you have an opinion," I said, mimicking his words back to him.

He smiled. "Nope."

Gah! No other person on the planet could make me go from laughing to wanting to shove them as quickly as he could. "Nope?"

"Everyone's going to have an opinion on this until you can't hear yourself think. Probably all different ones. But they're not the ones who'll have to live with your decision.

You are. The only advice I have is to tell you to take as much time as you need, and to pray about it. Harper's not going anywhere, and once you make your decision, there's no turning back."

My throat thickened. If we weren't driving, I would have hugged him the way I had when he brought Orion back. Which probably would have made him feel awkward again, even though we were friends now.

He squeezed my arm, quick and gone. The warmth stayed. "When you figure out what you want to do, if you need help with the *how*, let me know."

22

Two days later, as soon as the door closed behind me after I got home from work, Judith waved an arm at me in a dramatic arc from the living room.

"She just walked in," she said into her cell phone. "Hang on a second."

She made a *hurry up* gesture at me.

My brain ground to a halt. We had so many things going on I couldn't begin to guess who she was talking to.

What's this about? I mouthed.

"You'll see," she whispered back.

She set her phone on the end table and tapped the screen, presumably to put it on speaker. "Go ahead, Ryan."

"We found the stalker." His voice had that second-hand quality that revealed he was in his car on Bluetooth rather than holding the phone. "He was living not far outside Arbor, exactly the way we expected."

By *we*, he had to mean him and me. But then why had

he called Judith rather than me with the news? It seemed like he'd asked for me to be in on the call, too, but why not call me and ask to include Judith?

I peeked at my phone. No missed calls.

"We were able to get a warrant for his computer, and the IT guys tracked his Internet history. He was hacking into the pet ID company's website, checking to see if Melanie had updated her address. His obsession was clearly escalating. He was checking every hour."

Judith's eyes were wide. "Did you arrest him? He won't be able to hurt anyone again?"

The shake in her voice intensified as she spoke. I switched seats to sit next to her and took her hand. She clamped down hard.

"We arrested him," Ryan said, "and given his history, the DA is requesting the judge deny him bail."

Judith's arm shook against mine. I let go of her hand and wrapped her in a hug. She collapsed into me.

"We're safe," I said against her hair. "Bob's safe, okay?"

Her head moved against my shoulder in what I guessed was a nod.

She was definitely in love with Bob. She wouldn't have had this dramatic a reaction if she wasn't. Maybe she didn't realize it herself, but I should have put the pieces together sooner. The way she spent every free minute at the hospital with him. The way she hated it when he made a comment about being old.

Which was probably what was keeping them from

acting on it. Judith would never make the first move, and Bob probably thought he was too old for her.

Another problem for another time.

I focused back on what Ryan was saying. This was finally over. Melanie and Star/Tinsel would be safe, too.

Just one little thing still niggled at me.

"If he had the ability to hack her account, why did he want Star back badly enough to kill for her? The only reason to kill to get her back would have been to scan her microchip, since he wouldn't have realized it was defective. But he didn't need the chip number if he could watch her account."

Judith stiffened slightly.

Crap. Way to go, Zoe. You couldn't have kept that doubt to yourself until you could call Ryan privately?

The buzzing sound that signaled a car driving over the rumble strips before a stop sign filled Ryan's end of the phone. "My guess is he was hoping to return the cat to her as a gift. In his mind, it might not have been enough to get Melanie. He wanted to be her hero, too. Then he could create a fantasy where she fell in love with him because he rescued Star, and she'd never leave him because of her deep love."

Bleck. That was really screwed up. But it did make sense. Ryan had said the stalker was escalating in other ways with his obsessive checking of the website. He might have been panicking that someone else would return Star before he could. He might have even been concerned that, with how much time had passed, Melanie might not want Star back and might not show up to get her.

That ticking clock had pushed him over the edge.

"It's over," I said.

"It's over," Ryan repeated.

I continued to say *It's over* to Judith after we ended the call until she wiped her tears away and went to call Bob.

I sat on the couch, Orion by my knee, his head resting in my lap, long after I could hear her talking in the other room. It was over. It had to be. The only reason I still felt unsettled was because I had other things stressing me out. Plus, sometimes the body took a while to catch up with what the brain knew.

This was over. Now I could focus on figuring out what to do about Tonya.

***

My living room had turned into a virtual war zone. Judith was shaking, her finger pointed at Keith while she talked. And *talked* might have been a generous way of describing it. *Lectured* might have been more accurate.

Maeve leaned closer to me on the couch. "Did you give her the serum that turned that scientist guy into the Hulk in the Marvel movies? Or whatever turned Dr. Jekyll into Mr. Hyde?"

"Steve Rogers got the serum, and it turned him into Captain America." I whispered back. "Bruce Banner was exposed to gamma radiation."

"Whatever. Who cares. She's acting more like you than like herself."

I shot Maeve a *Gee, thanks* look.

She rolled her eyes. "All I'm saying is that maybe

calling us all together to discuss whether you should agree to visits with Tonya wasn't the best idea."

Maybe not. It'd seemed like the most efficient way when I came up with the idea. Let everyone voice their opinions at the same time and get a consensus on what I should do.

The best laid plans of mice and men. We were so far from a consensus at this point that we might as well have been the Democrat and Republican parties trying to agree on anything.

Judith shifted farther toward the edge of her seat, her glare focused securely on Keith, as if she were trying to force him to agree with her based on her sheer refusal to blink. "No offense, but you have no idea what you're talking about. You weren't there. Tonya isn't good for Zoe. She failed tests in high school if they happened in a month she had to visit Tonya. As a kid, she had stomachaches so bad the doctor sent her for an ultrasound. There's no circumstance where she should agree to visit her regularly."

A shiver ran down my body. Judith had noticed those things? She'd never mentioned them. How hard had it been for her to be the other child in a household like that, where I—however unintentionally—took so much of our parents' attention?

"People can change." Keith's voice was soft but firm. "We're supposed to forgive people because God forgave us. We're supposed to show compassion and mercy because we've already received them from God when we didn't deserve it."

He sounded a lot more like a pastor trying to counsel an irate congregate than like a boyfriend whose girlfriend was trying to make a major life decision. Not that he was wrong. He was absolutely right, and I'd never considered that Tonya might be genuinely lonely and regretting her past actions without knowing how to show it. Maybe demanding these visits was her version of a cry for help. Our dad might agree with Keith on this one.

But right or not, did he have to be so clinical about it? Like a doctor who'd forgotten that the patient he was treating was more than a diagnosis—they were also a person with feelings and fears who needed to be seen as an individual. Because even if Tonya was crying out for help, that didn't automatically mean I was the right person to answer.

Judith huffed out a breath that did make her sound more like me than like herself. "Zoe has forgiven her. But forgiveness doesn't mean you have to give an abuser access to your life again. Even Jesus walked away from people sometimes."

Keith said something in response, but it didn't seem to matter. Neither of them paused in their argument long enough to ask me anything or to let me ask any of the questions beating against the inside of my head.

I got up and slipped out the front door. If they noticed me leave, neither Keith nor Judith paused to acknowledge it. They probably thought I'd gone to the bathroom or to get a glass of water. Who knew how long it'd be before they realized I wasn't coming back.

I sank down onto our front steps and lowered my head into my hands.

Footsteps approached from behind me. No crutches, so not Judith. Too light to be Keith. A faint hint of lilac reached me. Maeve.

"I didn't think they'd miss me, either," she said. "Are you sure you can't force Tonya to give up the information without agreeing to the visits? Couldn't the warden take away her yard privileges or something?"

I snorted. "That'd be nice, but they don't do that."

"Well," Maeve let out a huff, "they should."

A lawnmower roared to life one street over, joining the background noise of Judith's and Keith's voices floating through the open window behind us.

Maeve lowered to the step beside me. "What's really going on? Why don't you already know what you want to do? You're not usually indecisive."

"Was that meant to be a compliment or an insult?"

"Merely a statement of fact."

I lifted my head from my arms. Maeve stared straight ahead, as if watching Mrs. Roszell across the street dig out her dahlias for the winter was the most interesting thing she'd ever seen. Giving me space while still sitting in the moment with me.

When I'd first met Maeve, I'd thought Sebastian had chosen someone as little like me as possible to get engaged to after our breakup. Like he was pointing out to me by his choice exactly how imperfect I was.

But as Ryan had noted when Maeve and I kept barging into the police station to speak to him about

Sebastian's murder, Sebastian actually had a type. Maeve and I both tended to quickly know what we thought was the right thing to do, and we went after it regardless of what other people thought.

Maeve had been pointing out how out of character I was acting from the beginning. Calling this friends-and-family meeting to discuss a problem was more like Judith than like me. I was more likely to call a meeting to tell everyone I had a solution to a problem and to delegate roles for that solution. The solution usually seemed so clear. Clear because I knew exactly how to act to take another step closer to the kind of person I wanted to be.

My heart felt like it moved up in my chest until it pressed at the bottom of my throat, threatening to choke me. I curled my bare toes over the edge of the front porch step. "I read a study once by a researcher from Harvard that said the people we regularly spend time with determine ninety-five percent of whether we succeed or fail in what we want from life. We become more like the people we spend the most time with. I don't want to risk becoming more like Tonya. I'm already stuck with her genetics. Who knows if there are genetic markers that make you more likely to become a criminal? Being around Tonya might activate them or something. I've already walked the line."

Maeve made an exasperated noise. "For heaven's sake. What you did and what she did are nothing alike. She committed crimes out of selfishness. You did the wrong thing, but you did it to help others. Saying you're like

Tonya is like saying a serial murderer is like Robin Hood."

The way she said it was a bit like someone looking at a fixer-upper and declaring it had good bones when someone else had said it was worthless and should be torn down. It was more grace than I deserved or expected. She'd taken a week to decide if she still wanted to be my business partner after learning that I'd fraudulently reduced medication prices at my last job. "So I'm Robin Hood now?"

"Don't push the analogy and get a puffed-up head."

That seemed unlikely. Most days my ego felt like a bike tire with a leak.

"If you give up on finding Harper now, then the bi —" Maeve cut off her sentence and glanced back at the front door, as if she expected Keith to have a sixth sense she was about to cuss. "You can't let her win. Yes, if you visit her, she gets the visits she wants. But if you don't, you're letting her control a major part of your life and Harper's by keeping you two apart. You don't have to be a little kid she bullies anymore. Don't let her take this relationship away from you over a couple hours a month."

23

Maeve punched the code into the panel to arm the alarm system on the vet clinic. "I don't need to come over to your house again tonight for a rematch between Judith and Keith, do I?"

I stuck my tongue out at her behind her back. So what if it was childish? "Hardy har har. No. They've decided to agree to disagree. Meanwhile, they both keep looking at me as if they expect me to side with them because they're both convinced they're right. The rest of the weekend was loads of fun. I didn't have the heart to tell Judith I've decided to agree to Tonya's terms."

She held the door for me, and we walked out into the parking lot. The days were already getting shorter, the sun setting. Pretty soon, I'd be walking Orion in the dark, even when we didn't close late. Thank goodness for street lamps.

Tyler waved to us out of his car window and blew a kiss at Maeve as he pulled out of the parking lot.

Maeve stopped beside her car, her keys in her hand. "Do you think I should give up and go out with Tyler?"

I fumbled my car clicker and almost dropped it into a puddle. The question was so un-Maeve-like. Had she ever asked me for advice before? Maybe she thought it was only fair to let me give my opinion on her life since she'd spent Saturday evening telling me what to do with mine. "Do you want to go out with Tyler?"

"No." Her answer was firm. "It's too soon, and I'm content on my own."

"Then why even question it?"

Her look clearly said *Do you really have to ask?* "He's refusing to respect my boundaries, despite both of us reprimanding him on his behavior. Either I have to date him or we need to fire him."

Crap. I liked Tyler, and he was a competent vet tech. But there was only one answer here. Maeve shouldn't have had to deal with his behavior for this long as it was. "Then we fire him. We're a female-owned business. We should be the last place a guy can get away with inappropriate behavior."

Something loosened around Maeve's eyes and lips, as if she'd been bracing herself for a different answer. "Thank you." Her words were quiet.

My throat tightened. I hadn't been the friend to her that she'd been to me. I'd been so defensive about my history, worried people wouldn't believe how bad things had been with Tonya. But then I'd laughed off how uncomfortable Tyler was making Maeve, minimizing her experience. "I'm sorry I let it go on this long."

She shook her head and waved a hand through the air, her signature for *I'm done talking about this*.

I hit my clicker to unlock my car, and it beeped at me. "Does this mean we can hire Kat back?"

Maeve slid into her car. "Don't push your luck."

I sighed. If Maeve didn't relent on that now, she probably wasn't ever going to. Maybe Judith would hire Kat to work at the shelter. At least she'd still be working with animals, and she'd be able to continue living in Arbor rather than having to look for a job somewhere else.

I glanced at the clock on my dashboard. Judith and Bob should be back from Judith's specialist appointment by now. Since he was still off work while his shoulder healed, he'd offered to go with her, even though she could drive herself. Company when you had to make a two-hour drive to the city was always welcome.

As if she'd known I was thinking about her, Judith's picture popped up on my phone screen. I swiped to answer.

"I'm just leaving work," I said into the phone in lieu of *hello*. "I'll be home soon."

"Can you come to Bob's instead?" Judith's voice was flat, as if someone had wrung all the emotion out of it.

My chest clenched. Nothing good could be said in that tone. "What's going on? Are you both okay?"

"We're safe. His pets are safe. But someone broke into his house. He would have been here when it happened if he hadn't been with me."

Dribbles of emotion were coming back into her voice

now. Dribbles that told me she was going to be in tears as soon as what had happened sunk in.

I pulled out of the driveway in the direction on Bob's house. "Is Bob with you?"

A pause. She must have shaken her head and then remembered I couldn't see her. "He's inside with the police. They're trying to figure out if anything's missing. I don't think anything is, though, because we didn't know anything was wrong until we saw the back door hanging open. Two of the cats were outside."

Her voice broke. The cats getting outside was far worse than anything being stolen. Things could be replaced, but if one of the cats got lost, there was a twenty-five percent chance they'd never be found again, according to the ASPCA.

I parked on Bob's street. His car, Judith's, and another filled the driveway, and two police cruisers already took the closest spots on the street. "I'm here."

I climbed out of my car and waved my arm. Judith spotted me. Even from a distance, I could see her posture crumple. I jogged for her and pulled her into a hug.

"I don't understand it." Her words came out muffled by my scrubs and her tears. "This is twice he's been targeted. What if he'd been home? Why does this keep happening?"

All the muscles in my shoulders and neck felt so tight it was a miracle I could still move. Bob wasn't home only because he'd gone with Judith, and she picked him up. His car was in the driveway when the intruder broke in.

A car in the driveway usually indicated that someone was home. The intruder would have at least suspected Bob was home. He either hadn't cared or he'd wanted Bob to be home.

Bob came out of the house with Ryan. They headed for us.

"It doesn't look like they took anything." Bob held out an arm, and Judith went to him. He hugged her to his side. "The TV and computer are still there, anyway, and I don't have anything else worth stealing."

Judith looked relieved, but my insides spun in circles. A basic grab-the-TV robbery would have been a good thing. Then we'd at least have a chance that this wasn't about someone trying to hurt Bob again.

I grabbed Ryan's suit jacket sleeve and dragged him away from Judith and Bob. What I had to say I couldn't say in front of them. Not with Judith barely holding it together as it was.

Ryan glanced down at where I had hold of the fabric, but he followed me.

"Nice to see you, too, Zoe." His tone of voice was dry. "Yes, I also wish it was under other circumstances."

I rolled my eyes at him. "We have more important things to think about than the niceties." I stopped when I was sure we were out of earshot and let go of him. "Is Melanie's stalker still in custody?"

Ryan glanced at Bob and Judith. Bob's arm wasn't around her anymore. What was wrong with the two of them that they couldn't see they belonged together?

Ryan turned back to face me. "He is."

"So it couldn't have been the stalker assuming Bob might have Star, and that he could salvage his plan."

Ryan shook his head. "We still have him on other charges, and he's still going to jail where he can't threaten Melanie anymore, but I don't think he's our guy for this."

Or for the shootings.

The words hung between us. I couldn't let them go unsaid. "I'm guessing Melanie's stalker denies shooting Bob, killing Avery, and breaking into my house?"

Ryan had his professional expression on, the one that didn't allow me to read anything from it. "He didn't seem to know who Bob and Avery were. He confessed to everything about Melanie and the cat because he didn't think he'd done anything wrong. He claimed he'd found Star, who he knew was named Tinsel, recognized she was Melanie's, but didn't know how to contact her. He was just 'taking care of her' until he could reach her. When she slipped out through a broken screen in one of his windows, he didn't know how to find her. He claimed to be watching Melanie's pet ID account out of 'concern for Tinsel.'"

Melanie's stalker could be lying about not knowing Bob and Avery, but everything seemed to point to him not being behind the shootings. Whoever had shot Bob and killed Avery was still on the loose, and they'd likely come back today, intending to kill Bob. "Are you going to keep an officer on Bob's house for now? This person has tried twice. They might come back as soon as you leave."

The look he gave me said *I know how to do my job, thank you very much.* "I'll put officers on the front and back doors until we can either find this guy or prove this break-in wasn't related. I don't want to take any chances."

24

I'd read somewhere that you should stand like Superman for thirty seconds before any important meeting or interview. Hands on hips. Chest stuck out. Supposedly, doing that would make you feel more confident.

I held that pose for a full minute in the parking lot of the Women's Correctional Facility, and all I felt was stupid. The guard who monitored the parking lot cameras probably wondered what I was doing. Time to give up and go inside before someone came outside and talked to me about it.

Sorry, sir, I was trying to find the courage to talk to my biological mother again.

I went through all the security procedures and put my belongings in the locker again for fifty cents. I'd better get used to it. This was going to be my life from now until Tonya died or was released.

My throat spasmed closed. Tonya would be released

one day. That would be even worse. There'd be nothing stopping her from showing up on my doorstep whenever she felt like it.

The guard led me back to one of the plexiglass cubicles, and I waited. Tonya was brought through the door at the back. Her gaze landed on me, and her smile trumpeted *I knew it*.

She sat and picked up the phone on her side of the divider.

My hand refused to move to pick up my receiver. I stared at it. Tonya hit her side of the glass with her handset.

My breathing kicked up. The air didn't have enough oxygen in it. This place should come equipped with oxygen masks that would fall from the ceiling like on a plane that lost cabin pressure.

I tried to do my box breathing. But I couldn't breathe in for four. My lungs seemed to have collapsed.

Every month. To do this every month. To see her every month.

Was anyone really worth that? Harper might not even want to know me. She might not like me if she got to know me. I might trade away twelve Saturdays every year and have nothing to show for it.

Judith's tight hug right before I got into my car flashed back into my mind. She'd told me I was brave, but brave was the last thing I felt right now.

Tonya hit the barrier again. A guard moved toward her, and she held up her hands. Whatever he said to her, it must have been a warning that if she didn't quit, her visiting privileges would be removed.

If they took her away, I'd lose my chance. That chance alone was worth it. It had to be. Harper might not want to see me. She might not like me if we met. But she'd know I tried to find her and that I wanted her as my sister. That had to make a difference. To know that someone wanted you. It had for me when I found out my dad wanted me, had fought for me. I'd make this sacrifice to give her that. I'd make this sacrifice, so I didn't have to wonder for the rest of my life what would have happened if I had.

I picked up the handset. "Hello, Tonya. I'm here to take your offer. You tell me everything I need to know to find Harper, and I'll come once a month to visit."

"It's rude for a daughter to call her mother by her first name."

The words *You're not my mother* jumped to my lips, but I swallowed them. Camille came with me once, when I was required to visit Tonya. My dad had come down with a bad case of the flu, but I still had to go. That visit was the worst one. I called Camille *Mom* out of habit, and Tonya spent the rest of the time telling Camille that she'd never be my mother. Accusing her of awful things. Camille took it quietly, with grace. I'd eventually grabbed the phone from her, slammed it into the holder, and stormed out, ending the visit. I cried in the parking lot while I told Camille over and over again that she *was* my mom.

I didn't want to go down that path again and lose

sight of why I was here. "Calling you *Mom* isn't part of the deal."

Tonya smirked. "Maybe it should be. Or maybe I shouldn't tell you at all. I'd be doing you a favor."

Cold trickled down the back of my neck and over my arms. The only way she'd be doing me a favor was if Harper was exactly like her. No way was that the case. Harper had probably spent most of her life in foster care, away from Tonya. If anyone was going to be like Tonya, it was me. "How so?"

She leaned toward the glass and tilted her head and pursed her lips in a *don't play dumb* expression. "If you never find Harper, then all the inheritance will be yours. You sure you want to find her?"

Something itched at the back of my mind. But trying to grab it was as challenging as trying to get a tiny bug out of a glass of water. I reached for it, and it bobbed away to the side. "How did you know about the inheritance?"

"Your grandfather never came to visit me while I was in here. Not once. But he made sure to send me a letter, letting me know I wouldn't be getting a dime of his money when he died. It was all going to his grand-daughters."

She kept talking, but I was only half listening. Pieces of thoughts piled up in my mind. When I'd finally seen Grandpa's will, that's exactly how it'd been phrased. His estate was to be divided equally between his granddaugh-ters. No names. Danica Dickerson had asked him to give her the names of the granddaughters he knew of, but we hadn't been listed by name in the will. It was what caused all this trouble in the first place. And if we couldn't find Harper, then the money would all go to me eventually. Because he'd left it to be divided between his granddaughters. If I was the only one, it was all mine.

My mouth dried out, and my tongue rubbed roughly against the roof. Hadn't Judith said Bob's biological father was wealthy? He'd passed away just before Bob found his biological family. And he had half-siblings.

If Bob's biological father hadn't named his successors in his will, but had only said that everything should be divided equally between his children, then Bob would stand to inherit a large sum when the estate was settled. That was money his half-siblings wouldn't inherit anymore.

People killed over a lot less.

I slapped the plexiglass on my side even though it reeked much too much of acting just like Tonya.

She stopped mid-sentence.

I pointed a finger at her. "Harper's information now, or I walk out of here and you'll never see me again."

I didn't have time to listen to Tonya any more today. I needed to get back to Arbor and talk to Bob. Because if I was right, the person who'd shot him wasn't going to stop coming after him until he was dead.

25

A uniformed officer stood inside the shelter's door when I arrived, guarding Bob the way Ryan promised. Bob and Judith were both sitting behind the shelter's long curved reception desk.

Tonya's visits were going to interrupt my ability to volunteer at the shelter on Saturday mornings, too. But at least I had Harper's information already sent to my grandpa's lawyer, and I'd be able to call Children's Aid on Monday.

A few people milled about in front of the glass window into the kitten room. I couldn't exactly blurt out my theory in front of them. Well, I could, but Judith certainly wouldn't thank me for it.

I headed for the office, motioning them both to follow me. The room was barely big enough for the three of us and the desk and filing cabinets. The smell of breakfast burritos lingered, telling me exactly what they'd treated themselves to that morning.

I quickly filled them in on my visit with Tonya and what she'd said. "So I was thinking that the attack on Bob and the break-in at his house might have been someone trying to make sure he didn't receive any of the inheritance."

Bob looked like I'd thrown a glass of water in his face —that mouth-open, eyes-wide, *I can't believe you did that* expression. "They've never even spoken to me. Or responded when I tried to contact them."

Judith held both hands to her chest, as if she were holding her heart in place. "Maybe you could tell them that you'll give them your share as soon as it's settled."

She had to be kidding.

"Give it back?" My words came out louder than I expected. I glanced at the door and took a calming breath. "If one of them tried to kill him, they shouldn't be rewarded for what they did."

Judith's gaze slid to Bob's face, then quickly away. "At least then he'd be safe. Better alive and poor than rich and dead."

Bob cleared his throat and pulled his collar away from his neck with one finger. "I wouldn't, though."

We both looked at him.

He shrugged. "I wouldn't give it back to them. I've seen what they do. Their profiles aren't private online, on social media. Neither of them needs more money. If I wasn't going to keep it, I'd want to donate it."

The look Judith gave him was the kind most people would have reserved for someone who rescued them from a burning building. Like she couldn't imagine a better man existing.

What kind of big sister would I be if I let Bob and Judith keep going the way they had been when it was clear they were perfect for each other? And that they cared about each other?

Judith would never speak first. She was too old-fashioned. And I wasn't going to try to change her mind. That would only give her a chance to forbid me from talking to Bob. I had to convince Bob.

First, though, we had to finish our current conversation.

I planted my hands on my hips, but that accidentally elbowed Judith in the ribs. This office really wasn't built for three people. I dropped my arms back down. "You shouldn't have to give it back to them just so they won't kill you. Whichever one of them did this is already a murderer. I'm pretty sure there's a law that says you can't financially benefit from a crime."

Judith swiveled around and cracked the door open. The people were now in the kitten room, clearly trying to decide which kitten they wanted. Hopefully both families would take two. People always thought that two kittens would be twice the work, but they were actually half the work. Two kittens meant they always had someone to play with and weren't dependent exclusively on their owner for the hours of activity a young kitten needed. Plus, they tired each other out, and their owners got cuddle time instead of attacked feet.

Judith closed the door again. "That's just it."

Bob and I both looked at her. "What's just it?" we said in unison as if we'd practiced it.

We both laughed.

Judith tolerantly shook her head as if she couldn't understand us laughing at a time like this, but she loved us both enough to overlook it. "This can't be about Bob's inheritance. They broke into Avery's house and shot her. Then they broke into our house. None of us are set to inherit, and Bob and Avery barely knew each other."

Fair enough. Those facts didn't fit my theory. "Okay, so maybe we have two separate people involved. Bob's shooting and the break-in to his house could be about the inheritance. Avery's murder and the break-in to our house might be a more run-of-the-mill robbery gone wrong."

Judith gave me a look that said *You don't believe that, do you?*

"Coincidences happen." My voice had a touch more defensiveness to it than I'd intended.

My shoulders slumped. Coincidences happened, but they were rare. We had a better chance of getting in a car accident than of all these crimes coincidentally happening in a cluster like this.

Which made Bob's potential inheritance an unlikely motive.

A knock came on the office door. "Excuse me?" a male voice said.

Judith opened the door. One of the families stood on the other side. The wife and the daughter both held a kitten in their arms, littermates by the look of them.

Judith filed out of the office, but I touched Bob's elbow to stop him before he could follow her. He paused, and I motioned for him to close the door.

The look of confusion on his face was adorable. "There's nothing I was holding back this time so I wouldn't scare Judith."

Voices carried to us from the front desk. We only had until Judith finished helping the family fill out the adoption paperwork before she started to wonder why we were still in the office.

I pushed the door shut myself. "I wasn't thinking that. Are you interested in dating Judith?"

That sounded a lot blunter when I spoke it than it had in my head. But maybe he and Judith needed blunt.

Red blossomed in two spots on Bob's cheeks like a child had swirled blush there. "You don't have to worry. I'm not going to act on it. I know I'm too old for her."

So I'd been right at least about Bob's feelings and why he hadn't asked Judith out yet.

I shook my head at him. "Ask her."

Bob's eyebrows drew down, casting his hazel eyes into shadow. They looked dark enough to be brown. "I'm fifteen *years* older."

The way he said it sounded more like *I'm a leper*. "So what? That doesn't matter to Judith. She's always been an old soul. Most of her friends when we were growing up were older than her."

The expression on his face said he was thinking about continuing to argue with me.

I crossed my arms over my chest. "When I was trying

to decide whether to visit Tonya to find out about Harper, someone told me to take the chance and not to wait because otherwise I might regret it later. Some things are too important to give up on."

Bob smiled softly. "Sounds like a smart guy."

"He will be if he takes his own advice."

He chuckled. "I think he might do that."

I opened the office door and let him leave first. He headed to the desk to stand behind Judith's shoulder.

I waved a goodbye to them both on my way past. At least if Bob and Judith sorted things out between them, my trip here wouldn't be an entire waste.

Orion would want a walk by now. Maybe I'd be able to put the pieces together for what was really going on with the shootings with some fresh air. Now more than ever, it was important to keep Bob safe.

I climbed into my car and headed for home. None of the ideas I'd had over the course of this situation fit perfectly. Bob was shot at the shelter, then the shelter was broken into, then Avery was killed, then our house was broken into. Star—I was never going to be able to think of her as Tinsel—had seemed like the link that connected all the locations. But she'd gone to Ryan's house, and he hadn't been attacked. His house hadn't been broken into. Though she had only been there a couple days. Maybe if she'd been there longer? But she'd also only been at our house a few days and Avery's house a few days. Plus, someone broke into Bob's house with his car in the driveway, suggesting they'd expected Bob to be home.

What was I missing? There had to be some other link

between the places and people who were attacked and the places and people who weren't. Because Melanie also hadn't been attacked or broken into since we returned Star. Ryan would have told me if she had.

Something must have changed between when Star was living with us and when Star went to live with Ryan?

I pulled into our driveway, shut off the car, and slid my phone out of my purse.

How long can you keep the officers posted outside Bob's house? I texted Ryan. *I'm sure whoever broke in is going to keep trying.*

There had to be a time limit on how long they could watch over Bob. All those officers were being paid to essentially sit around. Whoever was behind this might bide their time now and strike again as soon as Bob wasn't protected.

I put my phone back in my purse and climbed out of my car. Ellery was nowhere to be seen, which was a change. For the past week, since she decided to keep Avery's house and live there, she'd been turning the front yard into a permaculture garden. It didn't look like much now, but she promised to have plenty of organic vegetables to share next summer.

Why the garden was going in the front yard rather than the back was something only Ellery could understand.

I took a step toward her yard to see what she'd done today but stopped. Orion was barking so loud that I could hear him clearly all the way out here. He must need a walk more than I'd realized. I'd come back when Ellery was home and have her show me the updates. It'd be more fun that way anyway.

I headed for the house. Orion's bark was deep with a hint of a growl to it. Not his normal *I need a potty break* bark. Was Ellery working in the back yard today instead? That would definitely set Orion off, especially if she had workmen back there. Avery had never used her back yard. The place looked like a nature reserve with weeds up to my hips.

I unlocked the front door and stepped inside. Orion's bark was almost ear-splitting, at a volume that left a resonance echo in my ears in between. The sooner I could get him out of his crate, the better. He could go outside and bark at Ellery until he'd worked it out of his system.

I headed for the laundry room where we'd set up Orion's crate. A piece of kibble crunched under my foot.

What in the world? Orion didn't leave food. How did this piece get past him and out into the rest of the house? All his food was in sealed tubs in the laundry room so that he couldn't get into the food when he wasn't supposed to. But I had left the bag of cat food from when Avery took Star, that Ryan hadn't wanted when he took her, on the top of the dryer. I should put it into the trunk of my car so I didn't keep forgetting to bring it back to the shelter.

Still, Orion was crated. He couldn't have gotten into that food and knocked it over, either.

If he'd somehow managed to get loose, scatter food everywhere, and then get himself stuck between the washer and dryer again, trying to get the last bits, it was going to be a perfect end to the day.

I jogged forward and pushed open the partially open door.

Orion was safely in his crate. But he wasn't facing the door, waiting for me.

He was snarling at a man in a ski mask, his hands buried in the bag of cat food.

26

My body went rigid, my legs as heavy as if they were encased in concrete.

The bag of cat food! All the break-ins after Bob's original shooting must have been about the bag of cat food.

The bullet that went through Bob hadn't been found. He'd been in the back, where the shelter's animals were fed, near the cart of food. The bullet must have gone through Bob, ricochet off the wall, and landed in the open bag of food. Because the bag didn't have a hole, the police overlooked it in their search for the bullet. The shelter employee who'd fed the animals afterward hadn't used the cart. I remembered thinking they must have assumed they shouldn't touch anything yet. And then I came along and gave that bag to Avery when she adopted Star.

I took the bag back when Star moved in with us, but I didn't give it to Ryan. He hadn't wanted it. The person who broke into my house must have been looking for the bullet. The way they were when they broke into Avery's house. Avery must have surprised them accidentally.

Somehow that bullet must point back to the shooter in a way that the bullet shot at Avery didn't. Maybe when he'd loaded his gun the first time, it was before he'd planned to shoot Bob, and he hadn't worn gloves. He'd left fingerprints or DNA on it. He'd probably realized his mistake only once the deed was done. That would explain why he'd broken into the shelter after the police left the scene. He was hoping to find it before they did.

Then, when no one came for him, he must have known the police hadn't found the bullet. Finding that bullet before anyone else did would have been essential.

Shaking traveled through my body.

The man hadn't seen me yet, and Orion's barks were so loud that he hadn't heard me, either. I had to get out of here and call the police. He couldn't get away with that bullet.

I backed up slowly.

The man spun around and reached for his gun.

I threw my purse at his face and ran, slamming the laundry room door behind me.

I wouldn't make it to the front door. He could easily shoot me before I did. Maybe I could get into the kitchen and out the back.

The laundry room door was already opening. No time. I dashed behind the couch and dropped down.

If I could make him think I'd gone out the back, I could sneak out the front. My phone was gone now. It'd been in my purse, which I'd heaved at him without thinking it through. But I could go to Keith's and call from there.

What if Keith wasn't home? What if he was and the intruder followed me there and shot us both? Keith was former military. Surely he'd know what to do against an armed assailant. Though, he'd been a chaplain, not a combat-arms officer. But we could lock the doors.

Thank goodness Orion wasn't loose. If he tried to

protect me this time the way he had the last time I was in danger, the man would shoot him.

Heavy footsteps crossed the room. "Stand up."

My lungs collapsed, forcing all the air out. I hadn't tricked him. Should I have made a run for it and taken the risk of being shot in the back? Now he was going to shoot me in the front.

If that was the case, there was no reason for me to do what he said. The longer I could delay, the longer before he could go back to looking for the bullet. The longer I could delay, the better chance I had that someone would show up.

My throat went dry, and jitters shook my body. That wasn't any better. Then he could shoot them, too.

I sent up a prayer that basically consisted of *Help*!

"Stand. Up." The man's voice was irritated.

And vaguely familiar. His faint accent. Where had I heard his voice before?

"I won't ask again."

Maybe he didn't know which piece of furniture I was hiding behind. Would he start shooting through each piece? People used furniture as blockades all the time on TV, but that didn't mean they would stop a bullet in real life.

I couldn't hide here forever. I needed a weapon or something. The floor lamp was too far away and too bulky.

Footsteps marked his movement again. I wouldn't stand up, so he was going to come looking for me.

I was not going to die here, on my hands and knees.

I crawled as fast as I could in the opposite direction of his footsteps, towards the recliner. My fingers brushed against something hard. Orion's heavy-duty chew stick. Not the best weapon, but it was the length of my forearm and hard enough that, when Judith stubbed her toe against it, she'd screeched so loud I thought she'd fallen and re-broken her leg.

If I could time my swing just right and hit the gun out of his hand, it'd give me a chance to run. That's all I had to do.

I gripped the chew stick. What was I thinking? This was a terrible weapon.

But it was this or nothing.

I hunched at the side of the recliner, poised on the balls of my feet, ready to leap to a standing position. Would he be prepared for me?

My hands shook and turned slick on the chew toy. This was my home. I was supposed to be safe here. Just like Avery was supposed to be safe in her home, and Bob was supposed to be safe in his.

Focus, Zoe. You can do this. Lord, help me do this.

His toe came into view, and I lunged, swinging up toward his gun hand, putting the entire momentum of my leap behind the swing.

I missed the gun and hit his wrist. He screamed, and the gun launched back over his shoulder. It hit the floor and skidded to the end of the couch.

Still too close. He'd have it back before I could reach the door.

I leaped onto and over the furniture the way I used to

get in trouble for doing as a kid. The couch nearly tipped with my weight. I went down hard on one knee. Pain arced in a burning line up and down my leg.

No stopping. I stop, I die.

I gritted my teeth, grabbed the gun from the floor, and pivoted in the direction of the front door.

A heavy weight slammed into me from behind. I went down without enough time to even brace myself. My shoulder cracked against the floor, and the gun skidded out of my grip. It hit the far wall and came to a stop.

The man rolled me onto my back before I could get enough air in my lungs or sensation back in my arm to stop him.

His hands were on my throat, his thumbs digging into my windpipe. I couldn't scream.

The pain alone brought spots to my eyes.

My brain seemed to disconnect from my body. I was going to die here. I was going to die here, I'd never meet Harper, and Judith would find my body.

I couldn't let Judith find my body.

No access to kick him in the crotch. Needed another vulnerable spot. His eyes? Couldn't get my arms inside his. Where else? Where?

I balled both my hands into fists and smashed them against his ears.

His grip broke. Air rushed into my lungs, and I shoved him backward. He lost his balance. I scrambled to my feet and sprint-stumbled for the door. Outside was safety.

The door flew open before I could reach it. I collided with another body. Too big to be Judith.

The person spun me around behind them.

"Don't move."

Ryan's voice. I blinked hard, and my vision cleared. His shoulders blocked my view, but his arms were raised, as if he were pointing his gun at the intruder.

"Zoe." His voice was harder than diamonds and twice as cold. "Do you know where his gun is?"

"Yes." The word hissed out. My throat burned. I swallowed and tried again. "Yes, I can get it."

"Without going near him?"

I made an affirmative sound and moved slowly around Ryan.

My gaze landed on the intruder. His mask had come off sometime during our struggle. Broad nose, hazel eyes, and mostly gray hair. He'd been in the shelter shortly after all this started, asking about adopting.

No. Of course. He hadn't been asking about adopting. He'd been asking what came with adopted or fostered animals. He'd been trying to confirm where the bag of food with the bullet had gone after he didn't find it in the shelter the night he ransacked it. He must have also gone through the files that night, and he already knew only one animal had left the shelter between Bob's shooting and when this man broke back in to find the missing bullet. Star. He'd had Avery's address already from the break in. All he wanted to know from his questions was if she could have the bag of food. He'd been weighing his options and deciding if he needed to take the risk of breaking into her house.

"Zoe." Ryan's voice was slightly softer. "I need you to secure that weapon."

Right. I edged along the wall, keeping my gaze on the intruder. Something in the back of my mind wouldn't settle. He'd looked familiar to me that first day in the shelter. I'd assumed it was because I knew him from before I'd left Arbor.

But now that I'd spent more time with Bob, I could see the resemblance. Same nose. Same mouth. Same eye color.

I'd been right about why Bob was shot and why someone broke into his house later. His half-brother wanted him dead. The part I'd been missing before now was why this man had shot Avery and broken into my house, too.

I gingerly picked up the gun. "I'm pretty sure there's a bullet in the bag of cat food in my laundry room." I practically had to yell to be heard over Orion's barking.

Ryan cast me a quick glance. "Did it graze you?"

I shook my head. "From when Bob was shot. I'm guessing it has Bob's blood and this guy's DNA on it."

***

I wrapped the blanket the paramedics had given me tighter around my shoulders and lowered myself onto my front steps. My shoulder and knee still ached slightly, but not as bad as they had initially, which the paramedics said likely meant I hadn't fractured or dislocated anything.

They'd offered to take me to the hospital for x-rays just in case. I'd promised to go if I felt worse or if the pain changed. No way was I going to the hospital by myself. Judith would probably make me go later anyway.

Shaking started in my legs and rode up my body. At least the danger was really, truly over this time. Backup had arrived, and they'd taken Bob's half-brother into custody. He'd had his wallet with his ID on him. When Ryan told me the name, I'd recognized it right away from conversations with Bob.

The crime scene techs had also found the bullet in the bag of cat food. If we'd had Star any longer or if I'd remembered to take the bag back to the shelter sooner, we might have found the bullet long ago.

Even without it, my attempted murder would be enough to put Bob's brother behind bars, and Ryan had seemed certain that the bullet they'd collected from Avery's body would be a ballistic match for the gun.

I lowered my face into my hands. How much longer until someone got here? Once I'd given my statement, I'd called Judith and Keith. Judith had to wait for someone to take her place at the shelter because Bob was out on an animal control call. Keith was doing visits at the nursing home, but he'd promised to come as soon as he could.

"How about I sit with you while you wait?" Ryan's voice said above me.

I nodded.

He lowered himself down beside me and wrapped an arm around my shoulder, tucking me into his side. The chill in my body melted away. He smelled like freshly brewed coffee and pine trees, as if he'd made a cologne out of two of my favorite scents.

I relaxed against him. It wasn't like the awkward hug we'd had months ago. This time I seemed to fit in this space. "How did you know I was in trouble?"

"Orion." There was a deadly seriousness in his voice. "His barking was frantic and angry, and he wasn't stopping. I knew something wasn't right."

A distinction that only a person familiar with dogs would have caught.

I glanced at him from the corner of my eyes, but he was looking straight ahead, not at me. "But why were you here in the first place?"

"Your pestering." He angled his head a fraction of an inch in my direction. Something about the way he held his mouth made me think he was tempted to smile. "You were so insistent that I keep officers on Bob's house. But Bob wasn't the only one whose home was invaded. Someone had also been inside your house and Avery's. I figured that there was a possibility that if the shooter went after Bob a second time, they could return to Avery's house or yours."

He jutted his chin toward Ellery's house, which was once Avery's.

That explained a lot. After I'd picked up the gun and gave it to Ryan, he'd told me to go get the officer from the car outside of Avery's house. I hadn't been thinking clearly enough at the time to wonder why there was a police officer hanging out there.

"We were short-handed, though, so I was going to fill in outside your house until a regular officer could take my place. When I rolled down my windows to settle in, that's when I heard Orion."

Who was out in the backyard now, happily playing. That was twice he'd saved my life. Forget dog treats. I was cooking him up an entire pound of real bacon as a reward as soon as I could get to the store to buy some.

The final police car other than Ryan's pulled away. The remaining tension in my shoulders ebbed. That was the end of it. Bob's half-brother and Melanie's stalker would go to prison, and I could go back to my life. No more investigating crimes. I had enough other things to handle.

I sucked a long, slow breath in, and then let it out. Since we were here anyway, I might as well tell Ryan about the decision I'd made. Had I gone back to the prison only this morning? "I went to see Tonya—my biological mother—again. I agreed to her demands."

Ryan's arm tightened around my shoulder.

If I could stay here like this, even seeing Tonya every month seemed like something I could handle. It was like the contact with Ryan let me borrow his calm and strength. "Every time I see her, I come away feeling small and insignificant and unwanted, and like nothing I could ever do would make me worth loving. I don't know how to change that. You said you'd help me figure out how to do it. How to visit her."

I shivered slightly. A month ago, I wouldn't have dreamed of sharing all that with him. He'd seemed like one of those people who saw me exactly the way Tonya made me feel. But he already knew the worst about me now—the murderess mother, the fraud at my last job, my bluntness, and my crazy pajamas. Telling him how Tonya made me feel couldn't be any more embarrassing than all that.

Or maybe I was in shock again. That *did* seem to take away the few filters I had.

He rubbed a slow line up and down my arm. "Never go alone, for one. Take someone with you who'll back you up whenever she tries to tear you down. The deal was you had to visit her every month. It wasn't that you had to go by yourself. If she can't behave, you don't even have to talk. You didn't promise to talk, only to show up. You also didn't promise to stay for a certain length of time. You have a lot more control than you think. Approach it like training a dog not to bite for attention."

A grin slid across my lips, and an image of Ryan sitting across from Tonya, giving her his withering glare until she stopped talking, popped into my mind. But he likely didn't mean himself. Judith would go with me, though. And Keith. And Mr. Clunes. And Maeve. Tonya would rue the day she made this deal once Maeve got through with her. If Ellery stayed and we became friends the way Avery and I had been, she might even agree to take a month. Tonya wouldn't have a chance to hit me with her barbs because Ellery would keep the conversation hopping in too many different directions.

I laid my head on Ryan's shoulder. "I'm glad we're friends now."

"I'm glad we're friends, too. Even if you cause me more trouble than anyone I've ever known before."

I chuckled and closed my eyes. If I wasn't careful, I could fall asleep here while we waited for Judith.

Footsteps crunched up the walkway. I opened my eyes. Keith stood in front of us, staring down at Ryan and me with an expression I couldn't read.

Not jealousy. Not quite. Not distrust, either. More like disappointment.

More like, even though sitting here with Ryan had been perfectly innocent, it might not have looked that way to anyone who saw it. And under the microscope of pastoral ministry, I'd probably set off rumors that would take months—if not forever—to quell.

Ryan dropped his arm from around me and stood. He motioned for Keith to take his spot. "She needs to be kept warm so she doesn't go into shock."

Warm. Right. That's why he'd put his arm around me. That contact had been practical on his side. He'd probably wanted to put his arm around me about as much as he'd wanted me to hug him months ago.

I glanced up. Ryan was looking down at me, a smile in his eyes.

A return one grew on my lips. I'd read it wrong. Not a practical brush-off of why he put his arm around me. An inside joke for the two of us, referencing back to when he'd pulled up in front of the shelter after Bob had been shot, and Judith and I were both clearly in shock and in denial about it.

"Thank you," I said. "For everything."

He nodded and strode away to his car.

Keith took his place beside me and wrapped me up in

a tight hug. "I don't understand how you end up in situations like this."

A spatter of hysterical laughter bubbled out. "Neither do I."

I braced for him to lecture me about how my shenanigans would reflect on the church or how, if we got married one day, I'd have to be more careful.

Instead, he held me tighter. "I thought, when I left the military, that I was done with having people I cared about being shot at."

"I wasn't technically shot at," I said against his shoulder. "Technically, he aimed the gun at me, then I hid, then I hit him with one of Orion's chew toys."

Keith laughed too. "You *hit* him with a chew toy. Well, that makes a little more sense than when I talked to you earlier. You were talking so fast I thought someone had broken into your house trying to steal Orion's chew toys. I was going to tell you that you should've let them take the toys."

I broke into stress laughter, and Keith joined me. We got a couple strange looks from people who passed on the sidewalk, but even Keith didn't seem to care.

―――――

"Two million!" I squeaked the words out. "Dollars?"

Judith nodded, up to her elbows in sudsy dish water. "His bio dad's will said that his estate should be divided between his children and his widow, who I guess was a second or third wife."

She handed me a pan, and I mechanically dried it. I'd thought my inheritance from my grandfather had been generous. It was pocket change compared to that. "Is Bob going to keep working at the shelter?"

"Of course." Judith's tone said that should have been obvious. "He's too young to retire. And we've already talked about what to do with the money. After he tithes on it, he's going to put away a chunk for retirement and some in case he wants a bigger house one day."

Her cheeks turned pink. There could be only one motivation for Bob wanting a bigger house, and that would be if he and Judith got married and started a family. Which would have seemed weird to consider for any other couple who'd only had one date so far, but Bob and Judith had been close for years already. They knew what they both wanted.

"Then he's going to donate the rest to the shelter." She piled the last of the dirty cooking bowls into the sink. "We'll never have to worry about someone closing us down in the near future, and we can build that outdoor dog run we've been wanting."

Judith and Bob reminded me of Jane and Bingley in *Pride and Prejudice* with their goodness and sweetness.

Judith waved a rubber-gloved hand at me, splattering me with water. "I'll finish up. You need to hurry if you're going to call Children's Aid before they close."

She was right. I didn't want to wait even another day to get the process started for finding Harper. It'd been torture enough to wait through the weekend. I dropped the dish cloth on the counter, grabbed my phone, and headed for the living room. Orion lifted his head when I entered, flopped his tail twice, and went back to sleep.

Hopefully Harper liked dogs.

My hands shook as I dialed the number and put in the extension for the woman who'd helped me the first time.

When she answered, I told her that I'd gone to our shared biological mother and got Harper's information. I gave her everything Tonya had told me—Harper's full name, her birthday, and even the hospital where she was born.

"That does match one of the children we have in care." The tapping noise of her typing into her computer came though the phone. "I'll contact her case worker today, and we'll get the process started on a DNA test. You'll need to take one as well. As soon as we have a confirmed sibling match, that gives you visitation rights."

Her voice carried a smile.

I crushed the phone in my hand. My knuckles ached with the force. If I was going to ask my other question, now was the time.

I glanced at the kitchen door. Judith was singing hymns to herself while she washed dishes, the notes floating in the air. She wouldn't hear me. I hadn't discussed the idea with her yet. Or with Keith.

Harper was about to turn fifteen. What I was thinking would affect Judith now. If Keith and I stayed together and got married, it would definitely affect us and our relationship for years.

But I wanted to be sure this was what I wanted first. I wanted to know if it was even possible first. Like Ryan had said about my visits to Tonya, if I didn't know my own mind, it'd be too easy for others to sway me one way or the other. And it was me who'd be most affected by my decision. Me and Harper. If I knew what I thought and wanted, then I might still change my mind after listening to the advice of people I trusted. But they'd be helping me make my decision, not making it for me.

I reminded myself to breathe. "What if I want more than visitation rights? Like what if I want her to live with me? What would I need to do to make that happen?"

LETTER FROM THE AUTHOR

Thank you for continuing to support this series. It's brought a lot of joy to my writing because I love Zoe and I love allowing animals to play a big role in the story.

The next book in the Cat and Mouse Whodunits is coming soon. After a fundraiser for the shelter, Zoe and Detective MacIntosh find themselves trapped in a building during a blizzard with some of the participants —one of whom will die and one of whom is a murderer.

If you haven't yet signed up for my newsletter, please do. I announce new releases there first, as well as sharing recipes and other fun bonuses. I also give my newsletter subscribers a free ebook copy of *Sapped*, a Maple Syrup Mysteries prequel.

You can sign up at www.smarturl.it/cmilyjames.

Love,

Emily

ABOUT THE AUTHOR

Emily James grew up watching TV shows like *Matlock*, *Monk*, and *Murder She Wrote*. (It's pure coincidence that they all begin with an M.) It was no surprise to anyone when she turned into a mystery writer.

Alongside being a writer, she's also a baker, an animal lover, and a musician.

Emily and her husband share their home with a Boxer mix, nine cats (all rescues), and a budgie (who is both the littlest and the loudest).

If you'd like to know as soon as Emily's next mystery releases, please join her newsletter list at www.smarturl.it/emilyjames.